A GLEAM
GHOSTLIKE BALL

hung in the sky, trailed by a long streamer of foggy light.

"The Quakers brought this bad luck to us," one of the sailors screamed.

"Overboard with 'em," another sailor shouted.

The sailors' specterlike faces, bathed in the comet's light, reflected Nathan's own terror. He took a deep breath, bracing himself by clutching the railing behind him until his hands hurt. Would the seamen hurl them into the water? Or would their fear turn into rage, ending in senseless beatings—or worse?

BARBARA CHAMBERLAIN is a library technologist at Bradley School in Corralitos, California. RIDE THE WEST WIND is a sequel to her first book, THE PRISONERS' SWORD.

Ride the West Wind

BARBARA CHAMBERLAIN

David C. Cook Publishing Co.

ELGIN, ILLINOIS—WESTON, ONTARIO

RIDE THE WEST WIND
© 1979 David C. Cook Publishing Co.

Published by David C. Cook Publishing Co., Elgin, IL 60120
Cover illustration by Dick Wahl
Cover design by Kurt Dietsch

First Printing, August 1979
Second Printing, October 1980
Third Printing, January 1984

Printed in the United States of America
LC: 78-73150
ISBN: 0-89191-133-2

For my mother

EDITOR'S NOTE:

This story is based on the actual sailing of the Quaker ship, the *Welcome*. Its master, Robert Greenaway, and some of the characters in this story were real people. One of the author's ancestors sailed on this voyage, which was known to be one of the worst crossings to the New World.

Although it was not called by that name then, Halley's comet appeared as the *Welcome* sailed. The comet's appearance was studied by a well-known astronomer, Edmond Halley. He finally decided that this was not a special occurrence, but the return of a comet that had been noted at seventy-five year intervals throughout history. Scientists then had proof that comets orbit the sun and are a natural event.

Halley's comet is due to return in 1986. We will probably still be awed.

CONTENTS

1 The *Welcome*   9
2 Sea Serpents and Pirates   23
3 An Evil Omen   37
4 Comet or No Comet   42
5 Manservant   54
6 At Anchor in Downs   64
7 Pox!   73
8 A Floating Pesthouse   86
9 Lockup!   94
10 A Pirate's Tale   106
11 The Missing Cross   120
12 A Letter to Whitehall   134
13 An Unlikely Friend   141
14 Drager   150
15 The Hornpipe   160
16 Landlubber   173

1

THE WELCOME

Nathan pulled himself to the deck of the ship, fighting hard to swallow a lump of bitterness that was caught in his throat. The three-masted vessel looked worse up close than from the Thames River shore, when he thought she might be a huge, squat brown duck bobbing on the water.

"Why am I stuck on this tub with the old men, women, and babies?" Nathan muttered to himself. He should have gone with his friends Christopher and Matt when they sailed for America six weeks ago. He had not been that sick when the king had released his family from prison, telling them they must leave England immediately.

"Help me, Nathan," Edmund called from the railing. Struggling to the deck on a rope ladder, while holding a small cage and a large satchel, was too much for his little brother.

Edmund held the cage out to Nathan. But before Nathan could grasp the rope tie, the cage slipped from Edmund's hand.

Bam! It hit the deck with a splintery crash, two of the crude wooden bars broke, and a terrified black cat shot out of the opening. Dropping his own heavy satchel, Nathan chased the cat hopelessly, which only added to the general turmoil as the alarmed dark streak dove and dodged, upsetting sailors, colonists, squealing pigs, and goats.

The cat sprang to the quarter deck, but when Nathan climbed the steps, it leapt back down toward the mainmast. Finally the animal paused in the center of the ship for a few seconds, the short black hair on his arched back standing rigid. Nathan lunged, tripped on a coil of rope, and saved himself a bad fall by throwing his hands in front of his face so they hit the deck first.

Their pet cat, King Charles, seized this advantage to dig his claws into the mast. A nearby sailor tried to grab him but jerked his hand back with a howl of "Black Witch!" followed by such a string of oaths that Nathan hoped the skiff with the women had not yet reached the ship. The seaman's dark eyes glared hatefully at Nathan, a wicked scratch in the man's palm bleeding bright red.

Distressed sea gulls screeched around the top of the mast, diving in and out through the maze of ropes and reefed sails. King Charles yowled his protests, circling the empty crow's nest four times before deciding to climb higher toward the topsail.

"Stop! Come down!" Nathan hollered, knowing his mother and uncle would disapprove of his un-Quaker-like shouting. He yanked his hands, which were stinging from his fall, off the sticky coating of fresh pitch that covered the oaken planks of the deck.

Soon Edmund joined his shouting. "King Charles! Get down here."

Coarse laughter rippled through some of the seamen who gathered around the mast. Annoyed, Nathan wiped his sticky hands on his new breeches so he could tackle what he thought might be impossible—climbing the tangle of rigging to reach the cat. He succeeded only in covering his sticky hands with a layer of gray wool fuzz.

"I thought the king was in his palace today," one of the sailors jeered while the others roared. "Don't tell me he wants to sail on this royal barge instead!"

Nathan groaned helplessly.

Tears poured down Edmund's face. "I couldn't hold the cage any longer."

Nathan slipped his arm around his little brother's shoulder. "It's my fault. I should have carried it."

A young voice at Nathan's elbow offered, "Let me try to bring him down. Would you hold my hat?"

The possibility of help made Nathan feel better. He took a wide-brimmed, black felt hat from a Quaker boy who looked about thirteen, Nathan's own age, and watched as the boy slipped off a pair of brand new shoes, leaving them at Nathan's feet. For two months Nathan had been thinking resentfully that only he, among all the young men from the London Friends' meetings, had been left behind when the *Friends Adventure* had sailed the seventh month of this year, 1682, for William Penn's colony in the New World.

To see any boy his own age, especially one who knew his way around a ship, made Nathan feel brighter about the next two months at sea. When Chris and Matt had sailed with the other boys on the *Friends Adventure,* Nathan had begged his mother and uncle to let him go.

But all his pleading did not move his mother. She had insisted he was not well enough to face a difficult ocean voyage. So his friends had sailed away while he stayed behind to wait for the creaky ship, the *Welcome*. Even their dog, who went with Chris and Matt and Matt's father, must now be in America. The unfairness of it all gnawed at Nathan.

With admiration, Nathan watched the boy skillfully scramble up the rigging. The gulls screamed louder, like angry women cheated in the market, protesting further intrusion into their territory. Then their wide, white wings carried them out to hover over the water, debating what to do next in their own special language.

The boy ignored them. He climbed steadily, hand over hand, to the first yard. A light breeze whipped at his dark brown hair and his gray Quaker coat and breeches.

Through the puzzle of masts and yards and ropes, Nathan saw the boy's feet stop. He must have reached the spot where the cat had dug in, for King Charles meowed pitifully.

"He's near King Charles!" Edmund jumped up and down.

"What's happened?" Their mother and Aunt Marjory, Uncle Thomas's new wife, joined them in the crowd straining their necks to see up toward the main topmast. Nathan hadn't even noticed the skiff that had carried them from the shore reach the side of the ship.

"King Charles climbed up the mast," Edmund explained to his mother. "We saw the broken cage." Mother glanced at Nathan and the circle of settlers and sailors gathered around the mast. Even under the brim of her bonnet, a slight blush of embarrassment colored her pale cheeks. Nathan hoped the weeks at sea would give the whole pallid lot of them some badly needed color.

Aunt Marjory resembled a ghost, with skin so pale it reflected the blue of her dress. Some of the others who had been in prison several years had the same hollow cheeks and sharp nose and chin. The sailors' ruddy skins made them look even worse, but then the seamen had not spent months rotting in prison.

"Who is trying to rescue the cat?" Aunt Marjory asked Nathan.

"A Friend, a Quaker boy who must be about my age," Nathan said. *Friend* was the term they all preferred, a shortened form of the name of their church, the Society of Friends, not Quakers as the English mockingly called them.

"You see. I told you there had to be at least one other boy your age. William Penn writes he plans to have over a hundred passengers by the time we leave England." Aunt Marjory's

soft, green eyes and wide smile made her look so different for a few moments. Nathan knew she must have been beautiful before the cell door had slammed behind her.

He felt she was the only one who had understood the emptiness he had felt when the *Friends Adventure* had sailed without him.

"He's coming down! He's coming down!" Edmund pulled anxiously at his mother's skirt.

"He may not have King Charles," Nathan cautioned. "Coming in the dinghy from the quay terrified the cat, and then being chased all over the ship . . . he may not budge."

A murmur rippled through the crowd, proving Nathan wrong. The boy descended, using only one hand because the other held fast to the large black cat. Every few seconds a long furry tail flipped out in the wind.

Nathan breathed in a deep sigh of relief, not just for the safety of their pet but because this boy would be a companion on their journey. He rushed to join others who were reaching up to help the rescuer down the final few feet of ratlines.

The cat appeared to be riveted to the boy's chest. Nathan winced, thinking of those sharp claws digging into the boy's flesh. He tried to pry the sleek, dark body loose, but the terrified cat held firm.

16

His little brother broke through the crowd around them by crawling under a sailor's legs. "King Charles!" he scolded. "Come here right now!"

Before Edmund had a chance to stand up completely, the cat hurled himself into his young friend's arms, knocking him off balance. He sat down ungracefully on the deck, with the large ball of black fur in his lap. Edmund's hat flew off, made a small circle in the air, and then plopped at Nathan's feet.

The crowd roared with laughter while Edmund's face colored a deep shade of pink right to the roots of his fine, straight, reddish blond hair. Nathan and his brother both had reddish hair and light skin that easily betrayed embarrassment.

Nathan returned the larger of the two hats he now held to the boy who had saved King Charles. "Thank you for bringing the cat down. Are you hurt? His claws are like needles."

Smoothing his dark hair back, the boy placed his hat on. "That they are. Lucky I still wore my coat. The wool protected me."

"How did you get him to come to you? I never thought he would."

"I was eating a piece of jerked beef when the commotion started," the boy explained, "and I had slipped the meat into my coat. So I used it

17

for bait, and then grabbed hold of the cat. Once we started back down to the deck, it decided to latch onto me."

"King Charles hasn't eaten all day," Edmund commented. "Thank you."

"You don't know how glad I am you're here. My name is Nathan Cowell, and my brother Edmund is sitting on the deck in front of you. Where did you learn to climb the rigging?"

"I'm Samuel Tucker. My parents and I have been on the *Welcome* for two weeks during the loading. There's not much to do on an anchored ship, so I climbed the rigging whenever I was allowed."

Nathan introduced Samuel to his mother and aunt and the rest of his family. "This is my sister, Jennett, and the babe she is holding is . . ." Nathan did not feel at ease when he finished, "My little cousin, Bridget." He had lied about the baby's identity, but they had promised never to tell that Bridget had been given to them right before her mother died of plague, alone and uncared for in a dingy house on the London waterfront.

"Thank you for bringing the cat down, Samuel," Jennett said. "This is Friend Mary Crispin." When Matt's younger sister, Mary, smiled, the freckles on her nose and cheeks danced and her deep blue eyes sparkled. Nathan wished she would take more notice of him. Sometimes he tried to think of questions to ask her, just to start conversations. This time it was easy.

"Where are your mother and sisters?" he asked. Her brother and father had sailed earlier on the *Friends Adventure* to clear forested land in Penn's new colony.

"They'll be coming on the last dinghy with your uncle," she answered; then she turned immediately to Samuel. "You climb the rigging like a sailor."

Nathan felt deserted. Samuel started to reply when a booming, "Back to your tasks, men! Did we give you the day off?" made most of the seamen scatter, thoughtlessly and roughly pushing the settlers aside.

Two men strode through the crowd. The first one, who barked orders, limped slightly, but had the widest, most muscular shoulders Nathan had ever seen. He understood from the way the seamen acted that the two men were the first mate and the captain. The man with the limp appeared older. His whitish gray hair was tied back behind his neck, revealing a gold wire that was looped through his left ear lobe. Nathan forced himself not to stare.

The man behind appeared much taller, but Nathan realized this was partly an illusion because he held his back and head ramrod straight. Nathan knew he must be the captain. Automatically Nathan sucked in his breath and drew himself up as tall as possible.

"Settlers below deck. Find yourself a place in the hold," the first mate barked.

Obediently the colonists picked up their satchels. Edmund struggled to his feet, clutching the writhing cat with obvious difficulty. Nathan reached to help him.

The captain finally spoke solemnly. "This cat caused all the commotion?"

"Aye, captain," one of the sailors who was still nearby offered.

"King Charles broke out of his cage, sir," Edmund explained.

"King Charles, is it?" A trace of a smile broke the corners of the captain's lips and a hint of laughter cracked the lines at the corners of his blue eyes. Then his deeply tanned face became serious.

All the settlers except Edmund appeared awed into silence.

"Samuel Tucker saved him and brought him down. The water scared him when we came over in the boat," Edmund explained.

A few seconds went by until the captain spoke. "He'd best get used to the water. Is he a good mouser?"

Edmund beamed proudly. "The best in England. He helped us in prison," his little brother continued innocently.

A shiver traveled up Nathan's back at the mention of their months in the dungeon cell. Though he knew it was wrong, he could not help hating those soldiers who had locked them away, only because they were Quakers who refused to worship at the king's church.

"We can use a good mouser on shipboard. I shall give him a reward—a bit of salt pork for every mouse or rat he catches."

While the captain had been talking, three seamen had motioned for the mate, whispering excitedly to him. One of the sailors, the one King Charles had clawed in his fright, pressed a rag in his fist to stop the bleeding. All during the conversation that seaman had flashed glares at them. In his time he had been clawed by more than a cat, for a white scar parted his dark, bushy brows from above his right eye to his temple.

The mate moved back toward the captain. "Sir. Captain Greenaway, sir."

"Yes, Warren?"

"Sir, the men says they don't want to sail with that black cat. Claims he's bad luck, sir."

A look of horror crossed Edmund's face.

"Superstitious fools," Captain Greenaway muttered.

"A black cat is a witch's cat—a demon," the sailor said.

Captain Greenaway's eyes narrowed. "Drager. You can't believe . . ."

"Everyone knows a black cat is a devil witch. Bad enough we have a boat load of Quakers. But not a black cat, too." Drager's words split the air hatefully and thumped like a huge stone at Nathan's feet. He wanted to shout his protest, but no sound would come from his throat.

"He's just my cat!" Edmund cried loudly.

The captain turned toward the colonists. "I'm sorry. As master I don't want to begin the voyage with the men thinking we have bad luck aboard. The cat will go back with the next boat."

2

SEA SERPENTS
AND PIRATES

"You can't send him back!" Edmund cried, tears pouring down his cheeks.

Finally Nathan found his voice. "Captain Greenaway. You can't believe he is anything but a cat."

"I know." The captain eyed the three sailors who stood at the ship's rail, silently glaring at them. "If only he were any other color. Even if he had a white spot, or foot, or chest. . . ."

Edmund buried his face in his mother's skirt and sobbed a muffled, "I'll go back, too."

Their mother looked down at Edmund. Then her chin tightened as she spoke, "Captain Greenaway."

"Yes, mistress? You are the boy's mother?"

"I am," she said in a determined tone, one that made her turn from a sweet, gentle mother into a stone wall. Nathan recognized it though he had only heard that tone a few times in his life.

Deep down, she must be the most stubborn person in the world, Nathan thought. *The captain better watch out.*

"Captain Greenaway. You seem a sensible man. I find this unbelievable. The animal is merely a very frightened cat."

"I know," the captain repeated, "but my men are not educated, Mistress . . ."

"Cowell," she offered.

"Mistress Cowell, my men are the scum of the ocean—derelicts and worse."

Did he give any thought to the men standing right by him? Nathan wondered. But they did not flinch when he spoke of them in such unflattering terms.

"You signed with William Penn to bring my family and my goods on your ship?" she asked.

The captain's tanned brow knitted angrily, for he knew what she was implying.

"We have paid our passage to him, and this cat is part of our family and goods. I shall hold you to the papers I know you signed."

An exasperated gasp came from the captain. "I am not used to dealing with bonnets,

Mistress Cowell. I will speak to your husband when he comes aboard."

"I am a widow, sir."

The captain's eyes narrowed. "What are you thinking of? That wild land in the colonies is no place for a woman alone."

"My mother is not alone! I can do the work of a man!" Nathan burst out. Then he checked himself because his mother's eyebrows raised. He could almost hear her saying, "We do not shout, even when we are being treated unfairly." But a shout welled up from deep inside him as Captain Greenaway's now-hard blue eyes met his. Nathan looked away toward the shore, wishing with all his heart that he could fly there in a few seconds like the lucky gulls.

To Nathan's surprise, Jennett broke the uncomfortable stalemate. "Please, sir."

The scream inside him quieted as the captain's gleaming eyes shifted to his twelve-year-old sister. "I will help my mother, too, when we are in America. She isn't alone."

"I see that now," the captain agreed.

"I wanted to explain about our cat," Jennett continued. "You know we must leave England. When we were in prison, King Charles became a comfort to my little brother. The cat is like an anchor to him, like the anchor of your ship, sir. Do you understand? He's only six years old."

The captain's shoulders slumped. "You were all in prison, even this baby?" He moved toward Bridget wiggling in Jennett's arms. None of the colonists answered as Captain Greenaway looked from one thin, pale face to another. Though they had been out of prison six months, living in the dirty, sooty city of London had not helped them regain their color.

"Dear Lord," the captain muttered quite plainly.

"Please, sir, we Friends do not swear," Nathan's mother cautioned.

"Forgive me, Mistress Cowell. I did not realize I was." He turned toward his mate. "Mr. Warren."

"Aye, captain?"

"As long as I am to be captain of an ark with pigs and goats we may as well take along a cat." Then he turned toward the boys. "You will—must—keep him in the holds, away from the deck," he told Edmund, who nodded and sniffed loudly.

Nathan imagined the captain's words were a warning, for he felt the burning, hateful glances from the three seamen.

"We're cursed," Drager glowered.

"Quiet, Drager, or you'll feel your old friend, the lash."

Nathan started at the changed tone of the

captain's voice. Even the rough seamen drew back at the threat of the whip.

The captain faced Edmund, who drew as far back in his mother's skirt as he could. "And I warn you, we buried our last ship's cat at sea, died from I don't know what illness."

Edmund's blue eyes, ringed red from crying, grew wide, and he gulped. "King Charles is a strong cat."

"Thank you, Captain Greenaway," their mother said.

"Tell me that when we're a month at sea, Mistress Cowell. Mr. Warren will show you to the hold, and stay out of the crew's way, especially when we set sail in the morning. That means stay down in the hold unless Mr. Warren gives you permission to come up." With those crisp orders, he swiftly climbed the short ladder to the forecastle deck, the upper, front part of the ship.

Mr. Warren pointed toward the hold, and Samuel Tucker motioned for them to follow him. "Come on, Nathan. There's plenty of room now. You can make a place by us."

Nathan closed his eyes for a few seconds when he climbed into the dank hold, which smelled of fish and pitch. The resemblance to prison terrified him, and he dropped the satchel full of cheese rounds.

"Watch the low ceiling," Samuel warned.

"It's so dark," Edmund complained.

"We can't light lamps for fear of fire," Samuel told them.

When Nathan's eyes grew used to the shadowy hold, he realized they would have no privacy at all—unless they might hang curtains around the place they chose. But all their extra bolts of material rested in sea chests now stored in the bowels of the *Welcome,* along with tools they had bought, a chest of window glass, cooking utensils, nails, Uncle Thomas's books, and a chest of pipes to trade with the natives in America.

All they carried with them were their own straw sleeping pallets, linen, and extra blankets, besides the food necessary to see them through the voyage. Uncle Thomas, who should arrive on the next dinghy, carried a locked chest of silver coins—all the money they had left from the sale of his London home and their own farm in Yorkshire. At the king's command, the authorities had paid them only half its worth because they were Quakers. If William Penn had not been so respected at court, they would have received nothing. How Nathan hated the Old World.

Along with fresh food and vegetables, the Cowells had brought dried beef, herbs and spices, and lemons. Jennett and the Crispin girls carried so many sacks of oatmeal Nathan winced everytime he thought of the un-counted, monotonous meals that would pro-vide. If only they were able to cook the oatmeal . . . the thought of eating the grain raw made Nathan feel even worse.

Samuel led them toward his parents. "Mother, father, here are some new Friends, Nathan, Jennett, Mary . . ." He continued until the Tuckers had met all of them.

They had farmed in the country outside of London, Nicolas Tucker explained, and at-tended a small meeting of Friends near them.

Pallets and blankets covered the Tucker's area, next to a pile of sacks that must contain their food, a small chest very like his mother's, used for precious herbs and spices, and a locked money chest.

Samuel told his parents about the commo-tion on deck and the trouble with the cat. While he spoke, Nathan squinted into the darker end of the hold, recognizing a few other families from their London Friends' meeting, who had spread their pallets on the damp planks. With only their own large group, Nathan thought the area below deck would be nearly full. But he knew the *Welcome* would also pick up many more passengers on several coastal stops before they left England. Where would more settlers sleep?

"Samuel, the captain told us to stay below

while the new passengers came aboard,"
Nicolas Tucker reminded him. "Why were you
on deck at all?"

"I wasn't in anyone's way. They didn't even
notice me."

"We must stay away from the crew," Samuel's mother, Elizabeth, cautioned her son and
the new passengers. "They are . . . not . . .
respectful men." She looked down toward the
floor, hesitating to say more. Nathan agreed
that most of the seamen were rough and unfriendly. But staying below deck bothered
him. They would be crowded together for two
months, and if they could not light lamps, how
would they cook or stay warm? The ship might
be worse than prison, for here they would be
hopelessly trapped without anyone to help
them.

Nathan thought of suggesting that they
take the next boat back to shore. A heaviness
pressed on his chest as he looked from face to
face. He saw the same sadness and fright that
he felt. But they must stay here. In two
months they would arrive in the beautiful
new land William Penn had described to
them. Then they would be free.

Quietly, the Cowells spread their pallets by
the Tuckers. King Charles alone appeared
suddenly fearless in their dim surroundings.
He stretched out calmly to lick his paws.

"Nathan," Edmund called from the side of the hold. "Come here." The little boy stood in one of the empty gunports, peering out a large crack in the wood, which covered the hole where the round nozzle of a cannon would rest if this merchant ship were equipped for battle.

"We could see out if we slept here," Edmund suggested. "Then we could watch for sea serpents and pirates."

Through the crack Nathan saw the river and the houses crowded to the shore. The space on the floor below would be just enough room for the two of them to sleep. The wind from the slight opening might be cold, but they could always stuff a rag in the hole.

"A view and the fresh air will be worth getting a little breeze," he whispered to Edmund, dragging their pallets and blankets to the gunport. "And we might be the first to warn the others if there were trouble."

The familiar form of Uncle Thomas climbed down the ladder from the deck, followed by another family from their London meeting. William Penn, the founder of the new colony, would join the ship at the port of Deal. Nathan recognized the last person down the ladder as the broad-shouldered first mate, Mr. Warren.

"Settled in?" he asked in a friendly manner. Without waiting for an answer, he continued, "I came to tell you to stay below in the morning. We'll be setting sail, and you're likely to be hurt if you're in someone's way. You'll hear the creak of the anchor chain first. Don't be alarmed. You'll get used to it."

He moved toward Edmund. "Lad, I want to warn you myself. Keep the cat off the deck. There's plenty of work for him down in the lower holds. Do you understand? Drager and his friends would toss him overboard faster'n they would a bone."

Edmund nodded solemnly, managing a weak, "He usually doesn't go far from me and comes when I call—mostly."

"Good. The master's offer is still on—a piece of salt pork for every catch he makes."

Nathan interrupted, "Mr. Warren, when can we go on deck?"

"Don't ever, unless I give you the word. If a sailor finds you in his way, he's likely to knock you right over." He glanced at the gunport where Edmund and Nathan had spread their pallets.

"Good spot, that one. You'll see a lot from there."

"We're going to look for sea serpents and pirates. Did you ever see a pirate?" Edmund asked.

A strange expression flashed over Warren's face. "You'd better pray we don't. A sea serpent would be enough to handle."

Nathan decided he must be the only half-way friendly member of the crew. He gulped and asked one of the many questions that whirled in his thoughts.

"The ship's riding low in the water. Is she seaworthy?"

"Not leaking, if that's what you mean, and we have a good pump if she takes in water. She's loaded down with chests of nails and iron pots. We've even packed a whole mill down there. And furniture. Along with the barrels of water, no ship ever carried more ballast weight, and half our passengers haven't come aboard yet."

Bridget, who normally became shy with strangers, toddled right up to the mate. He swooped her up in his arms. "Whose child is she?" he asked curiously.

Dark curls poked out from under her too-large bonnet, and her dark, almost black, eyes filled her face.

"Bridget is my child." Uncle Thomas took the baby from the mate with a quiet smile. She did not look like blue-eyed Uncle Thomas, whose hair had been blond before the months in prison had turned it white.

"I know our ship isn't a beauty like your little Bridget," Mr. Warren continued. "But with all the ballast in her hold, she'll stay steady in the water, lad. I know her. She responds when we set the sails. She plods along against the strongest winds, not as fast as some, but as reliable a ship as ever sailed the Atlantic. She'll get you to your new land. Many a ship I wouldn't trust."

Nathan took no comfort in the thought that their ship plodded. He had fully expected it to waddle like a duck, taking forever to reach America, but how could a ship sail against the wind?

"Doesn't she need wind from the east at our backs?" he puzzled aloud.

"That's a good dream, lad, but that's not usually where the winds come from. You'll see. Once we're on the ocean, we have to sail against the wind, ride the west wind, because that's the way the winds are. Worse would be no wind at all."

Nathan felt a deep frown furrowing his forehead.

The mate tried another explanation. "You see, plenty of ballast, or weight, helps. If a ship doesn't have the right weight in her hold, she won't hold steady. The wind'll blow her right over. Steering is a mighty task, but we have a good master."

A bellow of "Mr. Warren!" echoed down from topside.

"The captain wants me." The mate climbed the ladder with remarkable agility, considering his leg must have been badly injured at one time.

Everyone tried to explain the happenings on shipboard so far to Uncle Thomas.

"I didn't think I had been separated from you for so long. It's only been an hour." Uncle Thomas shook his head.

After their evening meal of the flaky pies their mother and Aunt Marjory had made in the morning, they settled on their pallets to sleep. The lapping of the water against the side of the ship kept Nathan awake, along with wondering how a ship sailed into the wind. Slowly another sound drifted through the planks from the deck above—a voice Nathan thought he recognized singing a sea chantey. In a way it reminded him of the guard Christopher's lusty singing outside the prison. Quakers did not approve of music—too worldly—but Nathan had secretly enjoyed the young guard's booming voice.

From his nearby pallet, Samuel explained, "That's Mr. Warren."

"The man's a pirate," Elizabeth Tucker complained in a loud whisper.

Edmund rolled over and asked, "Do you think so, Nathan? He might want to sell us as slaves."

"Go to sleep, Edmund." The restless sheep and goats shuffled overhead as if to protest their new surroundings.

Nathan closed his own eyes. All he knew for certain was that he missed Christopher's singing. The gentle rocking of the ship in the river finally put him to sleep, his lids growing heavy to the mate's song:

No more the waves and winds will sport,
Our vessel is arrived in port,
Then come, me lads, a quick foot around,
While safely moored on English ground.

3

AN EVIL OMEN

A bright light, penetrating through the crack, woke Nathan.

Morning's come early, he thought as he yawned and stretched. Hearing excited footsteps creaking the planks above his head and alarmed shouts, he sat up stiffly.

Nathan peered out the gunport hole. Night still blanketed most of the sky, though the light that woke him glowed so brilliantly that a house or ship might be on fire. He shook his head. A gleaming, ghostlike ball hung in the sky, trailed by a long streamer of foggy light, like the bold slash of a giant artist's brush. He must be dreaming.

His heart boomed inside his chest. The cries and footsteps above grew louder. Most of the crew must be awake, staring at the sight.

So he would not wake the others, Nathan carefully reached out his trembling hand and shook his uncle's shoulder.

"Uncle Thomas, what is it?" Nathan could not control the quaver in his voice.

An eerie streak of light, coming from the brilliance outside, slashed across his uncle's face.

"Nathan, that's a comet. You must have seen the one about two years ago."

Nathan thought back to the time smallpox had struck his family. His mother, the only one of them who had not been sick, had said she saw a comet. Many people had believed that the frightening sign in the sky meant disaster. Since his father had died of the pox soon after and local authorities had seized their lands, it surely seemed true.

"The comet is an evil omen, Uncle Thomas."

"The timing couldn't be worse," his uncle agreed.

Though they were whispering, their conversation woke Edmund and Samuel, who tried to share the awesome view out the hole.

"I can't see," Edmund said as he jumped up and ran for the open hatch.

"Wait, Edmund!" Uncle Thomas cautioned

too late. Edmund's stockinged feet had disappeared above. Nathan and Samuel raced up the ladder after him, followed by the other colonists, who were now awake.

They huddled together on deck, staring up at the heavens. Behind the bright glowing ball, a long trail of ghostly light stretched out, gleaming in the predawn sky. Nathan followed the terrifying omen in its slow, deliberate path across the horizon. With a cold chill in the pit of his stomach, Nathan moved toward the railing to brace his shaking hands. Some minutes went by before he realized he stood next to the ship's master.

In the unnatural light from the sky, Captain Greenaway's face looked more drawn and lined than Nathan remembered. Obviously the comet awed even the self-assured captain, for the muscles in his chin and cheeks were tautly flexed. Even the tethered sheep and goats bleated loudly, straining at their ropes futilely.

Nathan sensed that the other men felt powerless, too—as if some dreadful force now controlled the world. The apparition had struck the Quaker men and women with such dread that they were hatless, for the first time Nathan could remember. The women's long hair fell loosely at their shoulders, glinting in the false moonlight. Everything around

Nathan seemed unnatural, the result of some villainous caprice. If there were a devil, as Nathan had been told, he seemed to be present now.

Suddenly, one of the sailors screamed into the silence, "The Quakers brought this bad luck to us!"

Captain Greenaway whirled toward him.

"We can't sail, capt'n!" another man cried.

The sailors gathered around their master. Nathan found himself trapped against the railing by the press of men.

Captain Greenaway answered quietly, "Comets have lit the heavens before."

"Capt'n! Somethin' terrible will happen. Don't set sail!" The sailor sounded like a terrified child.

"We've been a month loading this ship and are due in Deal soon. We have to sail," Captain Greenaway explained firmly. "Do you think these other ships will stay in port?" Nathan's eyes followed Greenaway's hand pointing toward the skeleton-bare masts of the many anchored ships.

"Then put off the Quakers!" Drager's shout cut through the crowd. "Overboard with 'em!"

Nathan shook with fright—growing angry at the same time. Why were they always blamed for everything bad that happened? The water of the Thames lapped against the side of the ship farther down than he imagined. Nathan was afraid of the hazardous plunge and the deep flowing river.

"Quiet!" the captain ordered. "If we put off the Quakers, we put off their goods. Don't you realize that? And there's no pay until the end of the voyage."

The sailors' specterlike faces, bathed in the comet's light, reflected Nathan's own terror. He could not get away! There was nowhere to hide from the hysterical seamen.

He saw his uncle and another Friend, Dennis Rochford, motioning for the women and children to climb below. Then the men bravely formed a ring around the hatch.

Not one of the men would be a match for any of the rough sailors, and, since Friends did not believe in fighting, they would be swept aside in seconds. Nathan saw Samuel's father motion his reluctant son below.

Don't forget me, Nathan wanted to shout, but the words died deep in his chest, long before they ever reached his throat. His heart raced wildly now. He took a deep breath, bracing himself by clutching the railing behind him until his hands hurt. Would the seamen hurl them into the water? Or would their fear turn into rage, ending in senseless beating— and maybe even murder?

41

4

COMET OR NO COMET

"I needs me wages, men," one heavy-set sailor yelled above the others. "If we don't keep these Quakers onboard, we don't get paid."

"Yeah, me wife's havin' a baby," a young sailor at his side added. "He's right. Let 'em go for now." Others murmured their agreement over the angry rumblings.

"Back to your berths, men!" the captain ordered quickly, seizing his opportunity to regain control.

The crack of a lash stung through the dawn. "Back, you dogs!" The powerful Mr. Warren, who had climbed down from the crow's nest, broke through the crowd, his whip biting out in sharp cracks. Nathan jerked with each lash, but the unfortunate sailors whose backs lay in Warren's path fell over each other trying to tumble out of the way.

Nathan gulped in fear. The mate had changed to a completely different man than the one who had held Bridget in his arms. Sweat poured down his leathery face and his eyes burned.

"You heard the master! Back to your berths, you scum!"

Some of the men scampered away, but most stayed, more frightened of the comet than the whip.

Warren stood to face the crowd in front of him threateningly. The men fell back toward the mainmast.

Captain Greenaway, seemingly unafraid of the men, announced. "We weigh anchor at dawn. Any man who wants to leave go now. I will sail this ship for I have bound my word—sign or no sign. Edwards, Browne, row the skiff to shore with men who want to leave."

Mr. Warren added, "You men see if you find a fairer captain before any mast, or one who knows the sea better. Some would as soon put you on half rations as look at you. Some would have you lashed for darin' to give your own orders on ship."

"The mate's right," agreed the same man who had said he needed his wages. "I've sailed with some keel-haulin' masters."

At last two fearful sailors—one of them a friend of Drager's—climbed into the skiff with the men who were to row. Nathan's heart followed the small boat as it moved between the anchor ropes of the other ships. Most of him wanted to go ashore. The Quakers did not belong here where the lash ruled, but they had no choice. If they stayed in England, they would either be sent to prison or killed.

"We can manage without 'em," Warren assured the captain as the skiff neared the shore; then he asked Nathan, "Maybe you can do some sailorin'. The Tucker lad can. Are you all right?"

Nathan did not answer. His eyes followed as the comet slowly vanished in the lightening dawn.

"Have you never seen one?" the captain asked.

Nathan shook his head and swallowed hard.

"There have been comets before, and the world has not stopped," Captain Greenaway assured him. Nathan did not mention what had happened when his mother had seen the comet.

"Such a sign is a mark of terror for men's hearts, though. The heavens are angry." Warren wound his whip tightly around the handle and tucked it in his sash.

"England fell at the sign of a comet," Nathan reminded the captain.

"But the comet was a lucky sign for William the Conquerer, wasn't it, lad?" The captain gave Nathan's shoulder a friendly cuff. "Depends whose side you're on, doesn't it now? Who taught you all that history, anyway?"

"My uncle taught us to read when we came to live with him after my father died. He even taught my sister, though I don't know why."

"You're lucky. I can't read," Warren commented—enviously, Nathan thought. "Go below now. You have to be out of the way when we haul up the anchor and unfurl the sails."

Until he felt a gentle hand on his shoulder, Nathan had not noticed that Uncle Thomas was behind him.

The captain spoke to them both. "Tell your people you will have to stay below most of the time we are sailing for Deal. We'll be closing the hatches."

"Thank you, my Friend," Uncle Thomas answered.

The master's eyebrows raised at this form of address, used only to signify someone who was a Quaker. For a moment Nathan thought the captain might bellow out that he was the ship's master, not a Friend. But he nodded

45

silently to dismiss them and then turned to give Warren orders.

Nathan's uncle and the captain must be about the same age, but they were as different as two men could possibly be. Nathan would never forget the combined strength of the captain and the mate when his whip had stilled the crowd of fearful seamen.

Even though the men were unfriendly, Nathan wanted to stay on deck instead of climbing back into the musty hold. Already some of the sailors had settled back in the bow of the ship, trying to catch a few more minutes of sleep right on deck. Others sat on coils of rope, still angrily muttering.

Even below in the hold, the confused, unhappy murmuring of the women filled the gray dimness. Tiny Bridget was the only settler still sleeping. Nathan looked down at her peaceful face and even, heavy breathing. A part of the golden chain and cross that she had been wearing when the Cowells found her had slipped out of the neck of her dress. Quickly Nathan tucked the cross away so no one would see.

"I did not think Quakers used such symbols."

Nathan started, staring up into the pudgy face of a new passenger who was not a Friend. His clothes did not mark him as a tradesman, or a carpenter, or a farmer.

"This . . . is . . . an heirloom," Nathan lied.

Even in the dim light, the man's nose shone a deep shade of pink, the rosy look of a jovial personality.

"Colin MacKay at your service." The stranger swept his feathered hat down with a regal bow, revealing a balding head.

Nathan wished the man had not seen the baby's cross. His sister, Jennett, proudly wore a duplicate but she wore it hidden. Nathan knew the crosses would buy a great deal, but the Cowells would never sell them. The necklace had been given to his sister by the mysterious man who had come with William Penn to save them from prison.

That man had known something about the baby. But Nathan could not understand why he would let Bridget go to the New World with Quakers if he were a relative or her father.

Both Nathan and the stranger, Colin Mac-Kay, joined the circle of men, now composed enough to have their hats safely back on their heads. Nathan did not bother with his.

"Sailing under such a bad omen is foolish," Dennis Rochford warned. "But I must go. I've sold everything. All the goods I own are in the lower hold."

"If we go ashore, many of us will get no farther than Newgate Prison," another

Friend reminded the group. "King Charles wants us out of the way. If the captain is willing to sail, what choice have we?"

Uncle Thomas, who had remained silent throughout the conversation, answered simply, "None. We must pray for the Lord to be with us."

"Plus a fair wind," remarked a passenger who managed a joke to break the tension.

John West, who was also not a Friend, added, "Without that we'll never leave the coast."

Nathan remembered Mr. Warren's words about no wind at all.

Suddenly the hatch doors slammed, plunging the hold into semidarkness. Nathan glanced up at the beams of light coming feebly through the edges of the square, closed hatch. He felt like a tiny bug, fatally trapped by a gigantic hand.

Quietly the colonists moved to their pallets. Most of them dug into their sacks for some fresh food. Nathan's mother gave them some tart, juicy green apples.

But Nathan couldn't eat.

Instead he dropped the apple into his hat, which still rested upside down on his pallet.

"What happened up there?" Samuel asked him curiously.

Nathan explained over the creak of the

48

windlass that loudly announced the hauling up of the anchor and chain.

From the deck above the sailors chanted, "Haul together, lads, haul."

Over and over the words were repeated. Every once in a while Warren's voice rose above the others, keeping the rhythm going. Finally the ear-shattering creaking stopped, and Warren cried, "Tumble up there and unfurl the sails!"

Nathan waited for what seemed hours. "Nothing's happened!" he said.

"Wait," Uncle Thomas answered him. "The sails must be shaken out."

Soon he felt short, forward jerks along with the regular, gentle rock of the ship. Slowly, then more and more steadily, they moved forward.

He and Edmund and Samuel pressed their heads together to look out the small crack in the gunport.

"The houses are moving!" Edmund informed the other settlers.

"Larboard the tiller, helmsman! Steady, now steady," the captain shouted to the man who controlled the rudder and steered the ship.

The captain had sailed as he promised— comet or no comet. Nathan was beginning to trust him and Mr. Warren, but not the rest of the crew. Maybe they would be treated with more respect when the founder of their colony, William Penn, came aboard at Deal.

But Nathan sensed no difference in the sailors' attitude when boatload after boatload of Penn's goods came aboard a few days later. The sailors treated Penn's belongings, and the new Friends who boarded at Deal, with the same abuse.

All that morning the sailors struggled with winches—swearing and cursing—as they tried to haul three beautiful, but terrified, thoroughbred mares and William Penn's white riding horse aboard the *Welcome*.

"The horses all belong to Penn," Samuel explained. "His family's very wealthy. The captain told me Penn will even have his own cabin."

The passengers who boarded at Deal were sent down into the hold. Nathan knew there must hardly be room to walk among the straw pallets now squeezed into that dark hold.

As the morning wore on, the waist deck, the middle part of the ship, filled with coops of chickens, ducks, turkeys, and geese.

"We have a farm on board, Nathan . . . a farm," Edmund cried excitedly. Even he remembered the days before their father died when they had farmed their own land in Yorkshire.

"They aren't our animals, Edmund," Nathan reminded him bitterly. With a quick flip of his hand, Nathan set Bridget's bonnet straight. The tiny girl had pulled the bonnet brim down over her eyes and was screaming because she couldn't see. Tending babies, rather than plowing fields, had become Nathan's fate.

"But we'll have animals on our farm some day," Edmund vowed. "Lots of them. And horses. I'll have beautiful horses on my farm—just like those." He pointed to Penn's thoroughbreds.

"We'll have oxen," Nathan corrected him. "They work better."

"Not me. I'll have horses on my farm."

Nathan had never realized that Edmund had thought far enough ahead to want a farm of his own. "We'll never be able to afford all those animals, Edmund."

Edmund's shoulders slumped, a frown settling on his lips. Then he straightened up. "I will. . . . I will have a farm with all these animals someday, Nathan."

Nathan shrugged. Stubbornness must run in their family, he decided. Suddenly he turned his head and looked behind the mast, his eyes making a swift search of the forecastle deck.

"Where's Bridget?" he screamed at the

others. How could she have disappeared with three of them watching her?

Edmund plunged for the short ladder to the waist deck, and Nathan and Samuel tumbled after him. Too late! They heard Bridget shriek, her screams rising above the jumble of sounds around them.

5

MANSERVANT

Nathan froze with relief on the ladder. Edmund stood next to the baby who was standing by the chicken coop crying.

"She stuck her fingers in the cage," Edmund began. "She doesn't know anything!" He had his arm around Bridget and was awkwardly trying to quiet her.

Bridget's mouth opened wider, and her protests rang over the water as Edmund took her shaking fingers. Unfortunately both children found themselves in Drager's way as he guided the winch, which was carrying a hooked barrel down the hatch.

"Get these squalling brats out of my way!"
Drager kicked out at little Bridget with a free
foot, but before his boot reached her, Edmund
grabbed on to him and clung tightly. Drager
let go of the rope, pried Edmund loose, and
tossed him hard on the deck.

Samuel swooped up the baby and Nathan
dragged Edmund out of the seaman's way. But
Nathan feared what would happen next. He
looked behind him for help. If Mr. Warren
hadn't been coming toward them, Nathan
wasn't sure what would have happened.

"I don't have to work with screaming brats
underfoot!" Drager screamed at the first mate.
The white scar on his forehead stood out vividly from his red face.

"I'll take them back to the forecastle," Warren said. "But I tell you this, Drager, touch a
hair of these little ones' heads again, and we'll
see if you can swim to shore—no matter how
far out we are. Get back to loadin'. The barrel's
swingin' free."

Drager glared at each one of them, especially Bridget. Then he turned sullenly and
caught the barrel.

Warren led them all back to the prow.
"Don't move from here," he ordered.

"Thank you, Mr. Warren," Nathan sighed
gratefully.

"Watch the babe. She could be over the side

in a minute if you aren't careful. . . . Wait." He disappeared down the ladder and returned soon with a length of thin rope in one hand. Swiftly he tied the end around Bridget's waist, handing the other to Nathan. "There. That'll be best," he said briskly. "Now, is your cat safe?"

"Down below in his cage." Edmund rubbed his arm, which was sore from hitting the deck.

"You're a brave one, lad," Warren complimented, stepping down the short, forecastle ladder. "Stay put, lassy Bridget."

Not until Mr. Warren left did Nathan notice that Bridget's golden cross again dangled outside the bodice of her dress. He tucked it out of sight, hoping neither Drager nor Warren had noticed the necklace. Nathan knew the solid gold cross would be tempting to someone who needed money. Three men on the ship now knew of the baby's treasure—Warren, Drager, and Colin MacKay.

"Bridget is always getting us in trouble," Edmund pouted, still rubbing his arm.

"She doesn't know any better," Samuel told him. "She's not quite two yet."

"We have to teach her," Nathan added, holding tightly to the rope as he sympathetically checked the baby's sore finger. Her red nose ran, and her cheeks glistened with tears as she tried to pull the rope away from her waist. But Bridget no longer wanted to go exploring. She stayed quietly with them for the rest of the day's loading.

Gradually the families who had gone ashore to buy fresh food and other supplies returned.

"We can go back to the hold now, Nathan," Samuel said.

Nathan agreed for he had to keep them away from Drager after the incident that morning. But the ship was so small, and they all hated the dark hold, which was now so crammed with people they couldn't move about.

When they walked down the forecastle ladder by the chicken coops, Bridget's tiny face clouded angrily under her bonnet. She examined her red finger and swung her hand at the innocent birds, scolding, "Bad . . . Bad!" but at the same time keeping her distance.

The boys laughed. "She's learned something, anyway," Samuel observed. He climbed down into the hatch first.

Edmund followed, his hat disappearing into the shadows.

Then Nathan lifted the baby down to them. The musty odor rising from the hatch made him hesitate. He wished he could stay on the open deck, smelling the salt in the breeze, the hemp ropes, and canvas. The sailors slept on deck whenever they wanted. But not the

Quakers. Nathan's nose quivered in protest as he climbed down into the crowded hold.

"How did the loading go?" Uncle Thomas asked as soon as he saw Nathan.

"There can't be room for another piece of furniture or barrel in the lower hold." Nathan described the loading but did not mention the trouble with Drager because they should have been watching the baby.

"One of the hens pecked Bridget because she stuck her finger in the coop," Edmund blurted out. He spoke too quickly for Nathan to silence him. *He should have been a town crier,* Nathan thought, *shouting news in the streets.*

Uncle Thomas gently picked Bridget up and examined her finger without asking when the incident happened. She rested her head on his shoulder and yawned. Nathan waited, but no more questions came from his uncle. Instead Uncle Thomas sat down on his pallet to rock the baby.

Why doesn't she nap during the day? Nathan wondered. If she had, they might not have angered Drager again.

"William Penn is not yet aboard," Nathan mentioned to his uncle. "And the captain wants to sail for the Downs tomorrow."

"He is coming, unless something has happened to stop his plans." Isaac Ingraham, one of the new arrivals, had heard their conversation. "Penn must take his deeds of ownership from the king to the colony. We thought he would be here already."

"The captain won't sail without him," said Richard Townsend, whose wife, Ann, was one of the women expecting a child.

"Anxious to sail?" Colin MacKay slipped up next to them.

"Yes," Nathan answered. "I want to get off this ship and onto firm ground in the colonies."

"We have a long wait and many leagues of ocean before that happens." Colin drew a large red kerchief from his cape, waved it with a flourish, then took a large, round, dark ball of chocolate from a pocket in his cape. "I have a treat for the babe. May I give her some?"

Nathan had never seen a cape with so many pockets sewn inside.

Uncle Thomas nodded.

Colin drew out his meat knife and cut a small chunk for Bridget. Wide-eyed Edmund stared hungrily at the piece given to the baby. Colin smiled, offering him a shaving at the end of his knife. The sweet aroma from the chocolate made Nathan forget the close air of the hold. He wished for some but did not ask. But Colin quickly offered him a shaving, too.

By that time Bridget had finished hers and

was reaching out to beg for more, a dark streak dribbling down her chin. Colin Mac-Kay looked at Uncle Thomas.

"No, little one." Nathan's uncle wiped Bridget's chin with his kerchief. "Our friend Colin wishes the chocolate to last the voyage."

"You'll have some tomorrow, my pretty lass," Colin promised, lifting his cape to find the right pocket for his chocolate.

Nathan saw about twenty-five pockets sewn in the man's brown cape lining. Some probably had money sewn in them, for he, Edmund, and Uncle Thomas all had coins in the linings of their coats. Either Colin was a magician, or he had ordered the cape cleverly fitted for the journey.

What does he do? Nathan wondered. Although Colin MacKay's clothes were made of fine wool, and that placed him in a wealthy class, he did not act like a nobleman. Nathan thought he seemed unusually friendly, especially in a world where so many hated Quakers.

That night Nathan lay on his pallet looking out the hole in the gunport. The comet had disappeared from the sky, and he felt thankful.

Captain Greenaway had left the hatch open to give them more air. And Nathan took deep breaths. He knew that the hatch would be slammed shut when they set sail again.

The ship rocked gently, but somehow his eyes wouldn't close.

Colin MacKay must have had trouble sleeping, too, for he came to the gunport to admire Nathan's view. "I saw you had a rope around the baby's waist today," he commented. "Good idea that. A little one might easily fall into the ocean and disappear. You must be careful of her," Colin warned. He almost seemed too concerned about Bridget. The way he spoke made goose bumps shiver up and down Nathan's arms.

Nathan did not answer or say the rope was Warren's idea. Colin MacKay's special interest in Bridget worried him. Strangers did not bother about what happened to toddlers, especially Quaker children. Nathan wondered if anyone else had noticed MacKay's unusual friendliness. Or was Nathan just twisting the man's pleasant nature into something that did not exist? He decided to change the subject completely.

"I wish we would set sail to the ocean. We've been a week and a half sailing along the coast."

"It won't be long now," Colin assured him. "Nathan, you may call me Friend Colin if you wish. I know it is your custom, and I shall do the same."

"You do not mind being in a shipload of Quakers, Friend Colin?" Nathan could not hold the question back.

For a second, Colin closed his eyes. When they opened, Nathan saw a wild spark in the flecked blue eyes, a strange combination of sadness and excitement.

"I have a change in mind, Friend Nathan, a chance for a new life. I have always been a manservant. When this chance came along, I took it. In the New World, I shall be a land-owner."

His words struck Nathan as sincere. The chance to own land drew many who had no opportunity in the Old World, where a man-servant would remain a manservant all his life. He had been too suspicious. After all the young prison guard Christopher had saved their lives, and he was not a Quaker.

With a grand sweep, Colin wrapped his new cloak around himself, carefully stepping between pallets until he reached his own. Then all was quiet.

Once during the night, Nathan heard louder voices on deck, and he thought a boat must have come alongside. William Penn might have arrived at last. Nathan wished he could climb the ladder and stroll the deck whenever he wanted. He dared not. Captain Greenaway had already warned them never to go above without permission. And Warren had advised them to stay together when they went on deck because of the surly sailors.

Sometime during the dawning hours, the hatch slammed loudly. They were on their way to America.

6

AT ANCHOR
IN DOWNS

Most of the new settlers woke startled. All of
them were farmers or merchants who had
never been to sea before. The children began
to whimper, frightened of the strangeness and
the loud noise. Nathan's mother and aunt,
Jennett, and the Crispin girls comforted the
new arrivals. Those who had been aboard
since London knew what was happening. Now
the *Welcome* would sail along the coast until
Land's End, then head for the open sea and the
new colony called Pennsylvania—Penn's
woods.

During the day, the hatch opened again.

Nathan recognized William Penn, who climbed down into the hold, followed by another man.

Penn's Quaker suit was cut of an extra fine wool, and, unusual for a Friend, he wore a wig under his broad-brimmed hat.

The colonists gathered around to welcome him and the other man.

"This is Friend Philip Theodore Lehnman, my secretary." With his characteristic friendliness, Penn greeted everyone. Most he knew by name, even Nathan, Jennett, Edmund, and Bridget.

Then, in true Quaker fashion, William Penn organized a meeting in the hold. A few of the new colonists like Colin MacKay, who were not Friends, stayed on their pallets. But most gathered together, some sitting on their small wooden sea chests and others standing. All remained silent, "waiting on the Lord."

As always during a meeting, Nathan's mind wandered. The boards under him swayed back and forth, and he began to count the knotholes in the wooden planks. He had reached twenty when he heard Warren's muffled orders. He knew the seamen would be climbing the tarred ratlines up the masts and yards. Why couldn't he be out there, too?

Every once in a while a man would remove his hat to speak.

"Lord, we thank you for the opportunity to seek a new land, a place where we will be free to worship as we please. Bless us on this long voyage. Keep us safe and free from illness. And bring us finally to the promised land."

When one person was finished speaking, the company would fall silent again until another person spoke. Nathan wished to be outside, as free as the gulls gliding on the wind around the masts.

He did not hear much of what was said. He felt the heavy weight of their burdens pressing on his shoulders: the antagonism of the sailors, the hatred of the king, of everyone in England. He was still not sure their faith was worth the long, bitter months in jail and the loss of their farm.

They would have a new farm, though, and soon. . . .

By the time the *Welcome* anchored in Downs a few days later, many of the passengers were seasick. Downs was an area off the coast where many ships waited at anchor for a fair wind to set to sea. The ship no longer swayed gently, but bobbed up and down straining against the anchor, rocking back and forth until Nathan prayed for firm ground under his feet. Warren promised him he would get "sea legs," but his lower limbs refused to cooperate, trembling and aching in protest.

"I have sailed many times, but never across the ocean," said William Penn, son of the most famous admiral in England and a man who knew as much about the sea as Captain Greenaway. "I'm afraid this bobbing is a baby's cradle compared to what is to come."

His statement made some of the passengers even greener. Whenever they were allowed on deck, the boys scrambled up to breathe in as much sea-tipped wind and fresh air as their lungs would hold. The *Welcome* sat at Downs, waiting as were several other ships for a fair wind to sail west.

Finally two ships with impatient captains weighed anchor and set full sail.

"They'll never make the ocean." Warren laughed casually.

Nathan wiped away the moist salty mist blown onto his eyelids and cheeks and watched as the large ships were forced back by the strong winds, as though they were toy boats floating on a rain puddle.

I wonder if we will have to stay at anchor forever, bobbing and waiting, Nathan thought. When he complained of nothing to do, Uncle Thomas volunteered him to milk the goats because their owner groaned from seasickness in the hold. Samuel asked his parents if he could help Nathan do the milking.

This gave both boys more time on deck and provided fresh milk for the children. But as everywhere else on ship, there was little room to move about. Horses, goats, cows, and cages of birds filled the main deck around the hatch. Nathan narrowly escaped being kicked by the horses a number of times. Once he whirled in time to keep his head safe, but overturned the bucket. Goats' milk sloshed over his new shoes.

The seamen nearby roared at his misfortune.

Another chore he disliked was dumping buckets of garbage from the hold. The gulls swooped and dived and screeched at the banquet Samuel and he threw them.

"Aren't we ever going to leave?" he complained to Samuel one day.

"Look, Nathan," Samuel pointed. He watched another nearby ship unfurl her canvas and attempt to head to the open sea. The winds beat her back.

"She's too anxious," Mr. Warren explained to them. "Her captain won't wait for the right wind. No matter how he tries, he won't get out of the Downs with the wind blowing at us."

"You said we could sail against the wind," Nathan reminded the first mate.

A sparkle lit Warren's pale blue eyes. "I did.

At sea you'll understand. . . . Times like this, it's best to anchor and wait. Greenaway knows."

All the next day, they bobbed in the windy Downs. Most of the passengers became seasick. The effects of the rocking had struck the adults first. But now many children joined their parents, unable to do anything but lie helplessly in the hold. Nathan's head began to ache. His knees collapsed weakly, and he fell in his pallet into a grateful sleep.

In his dreams he always saw the brilliant reflection of the terrifying comet leaping out of the river Thames. This time the picture was broken by the slamming of the hatch and the cry, "Fair wind!"

He woke but did not get up, just lay there listening to the hasty, muffled orders and the thud of the anchor chain. The sailors' footsteps creaked the boards above his pounding head. He knew the canvas was being shaken out to catch the fair gusts.

He should be thrilled, his heart leaping ahead as he felt the canvas fill with wind and the ship jerk forward. But his head and stomach bobbed and rocked, sickening him. Again he prayed for a real house and a solid bed.

His uncle, aunt, and mother, and most all the other passengers, lay sick. For some reason, Edmund and Bridget did not seem affected. About every five minutes his little brother asked, "Do you feel better?"

"No," Nathan groaned. "Go away."

"There's no place to go," Edmund complained.

"Edmund," Uncle Thomas answered from his pallet.

"Yes, uncle."

"Edmund, we need you to watch Bridget."

"Watch Bridget? That baby?"

"Yes, Edmund," their mother whispered. "While the rest of us are sick, you must take care of her. You know where the biscuits are, and the water barrel. Keep her away from the hatch that leads below."

"Yes, mother." Edmund dropped to his pallet with a disgusted expression on his face and petted the loudly purring King Charles.

For three endless days sailing on the ocean, Nathan wished to die. The ship bobbed as much up and down and side to side as it moved forward. The stench in the hold made him sicker than ever. At different times he heard the sailors overhead—laughing, joking, dancing, and singing.

He hated them all.

After four miserable days, Nathan's headache finally disappeared. He had not been as sick as most of the others, though he still felt weak and shaky. Eating a biscuit and drinking some water made him stronger.

Edmund played with other children who seemed to have gotten their sea legs first. He had made a special friend, Josiah Fitzwater, a boy about six years old. Nathan's own friend, Samuel, was still sick and refused to even try a biscuit. Jennett and Mary recovered.

"Good," Edmund said. "Now you can watch Bridget."

Later in the day Edmund came back to sit on his pallet, sighing loudly.

"What's the matter, Edmund?" Nathan asked.

"My friend Josiah can't play any more today. He's hot and shaking. I took him some water because his mother and father are still sick."

"Maybe we can help him," Jennett offered, moving over toward the Fitzwater family.

She knelt over Josiah's bed for a few minutes, and then quickly returned to Nathan.

He saw what was left of her color drain from her face.

"Nathan!" Jennett swallowed hard and stopped speaking. Her next words refused to come, and her face appeared shockingly white in the dim light. She grabbed his arm tightly. "Nathan. Come over to Josiah." She pulled him to where the little boy lay almost completely covered with a blanket.

"Look." She drew back the covering.

Nathan choked down the sob that filled his throat.

7

POX!

A chill settled around Nathan's shoulders, turning the back of his neck icy. He shuddered violently, refusing to believe what he saw.

"Nathan, what can we do?" Jennett whispered.

"We can't do anything," Nathan answered bitterly. "He has the pox. Be thankful that we've had it."

"The others who haven't will get it quickly," she protested.

"I know." Nathan stared at the rising sores on the boy's face and neck. He rubbed the right side of his own neck, underneath his chin, where the worst of his scars were. Nathan knew that for some reason these scars protected him. He and Jennett and Edmund were safe. Was Bridget? She must be kept away from this side of the hold.

But he knew that was impossible. The hold was like one large room covered with a patchwork of blankets. It gave no protection, no place to hide.

"We can't help those who haven't had pox. You know that, Jennett," Nathan decided. "We will care for Josiah until his parents are better. There's no use telling them about the sickness when they are feeling so ill themselves. If I get the chance to go on deck, I will tell William Penn."

Nathan and Jennett and Mary took turns bringing water to Josiah. The boy's skin became hotter and hotter, though at the same time he shivered. Jennett gently placed a cloth dipped in water on his head.

"If mother were better, she could tell us what herbs to use."

"Jennett." Josiah's little sister, another Mary, called to her. "Would you put a rag on my head, too? It hurts. I feel hot, and my back hurts." She shook as though it were snowing but her forehead felt warm.

Mary Crispin took off the little girl's bonnet and helped her lie down. The same pinkish skin erruptions marked her face.

Nathan closed his eyes, then opened them, hoping to see the young girl with a clear skin. But the growing circles on her face almost turned larger and redder before his eyes.

The comet had cursed their voyage! What would the sailors do when they found out? Nathan dared not imagine. He was afraid to tell anyone, and prayed these two children would be the only ones affected. If any more became ill . . .

"Nathan," Jennett said. "Mary tells me her family has never had the pox."

"Then stay away, Mary," Nathan advised her. "Jennett and I can care for them. Don't take the chance."

"I have already been helping, Nathan," she reminded him, not moving.

When the hatch opened and the familiar form of William Penn climbed into the hold, Nathan could not decide what to do. Should he tell what horror lurked aboard? The captain might turn the ship back. After sailing for two weeks along the coast, anchoring, forever picking up passengers and goods, they had finally set to sea, and now this.

"Shall we tell William Penn?" Jennett leaned next to his ear to whisper.

Penn stepped from pallet to pallet, assuring the seasick passengers that their illness would pass. Soon he would be near them, and although he might not notice that the Fitzwater children had the pox, he certainly would want to give them some encouragement.

He greeted Nathan and Jennett first. "Good day, Friends. You have not taken the seasickness? Children fare better than their parents—except for these two small ones." With a worried frown across his face, he pointed to the tiny forms hidden by blankets. "I did not expect everyone to take it so violently."

"We have been sick, but not for as long as some of our older Friends," Jennett answered, staring straight at Nathan.

"This will pass," he assured them. "I've spent much time on ships, made many voyages to Ireland and Holland, and have been at sea so often with my father that I take to the waves easily now. My secretary is ill, though."

Jennett and Nathan exchanged glances. His sister's expression said, "Tell him."

Nathan drew in a deep breath of the putrid air. "Friend Penn . . ." he began, then lost his courage. *He must be told,* Nathan thought. The whole ship would know soon.

Penn placed his hand reassuringly on Nathan's shoulder. This was the time to tell him, Nathan knew. He bent over and pulled the blanket away from Josiah's chin, and the damp cloth off his forehead.

Penn dropped on his knees by the boy. "No," he moaned. "These poor little ones. How long . . . ?"

"Since yesterday," Jennett answered. "His sister, Mary, is sick, too. What can we do?"

"We will pray for the pox to stop here. I shall tell the captain privately." Penn turned and drew Nathan, Jennett, Mary Crispin, and Edmund close to him. He prayed that the Lord would heal the Fitzwaters and stop the smallpox from spreading further. Nathan wondered if their prayers would be heard.

When Penn looked up again, Edmund grabbed his hand. "Will you tell us more about the Indians in America?" A small group of children gathered around Penn as he described the Indians and the endless, rich forested coast along the Delaware River.

"You can reach up and pluck birds from the air with your bare hands, they say," Penn told the wide-eyed children. "But this land the king has granted me already belongs to a proud race. It is their land, my dear young Friends. We will purchase land for our farms and treat them fairly in all matters of business. I have written them promising this."

A week passed on the bobbing ship, and no

one else became sick. Even with their scabbing sores, Mary and Josiah survived the fever. Penn took turns with Nathan and Jennett and Mary Crispin nursing the two children.

"I've left my own family and young ones," he told Nathan. "My wife was soon to have a baby and could not travel."

Gradually the adults were recovering. Some sat up and others walked short distances in the hold. Nathan tried to insist that Mary Crispin stay away from the sick children.

"Nathan," Josiah complained, "my chest hurts."

Bathing the boy's runny sores, Nathan noticed his skin steaming hot and his breathing coming in difficult gasps.

"Breathing hurts," he complained often, his lips turning bluish.

"Jennett," Nathan asked, "is the physician, Thomas Wynne, any better?"

"Still too seasick to help," she replied. "I'll ask mother about herbs." Jennett knelt over where their mother sat, her back against the side of the ship, trying to fight the seasickness. Mother always knew the right herbs for nursing the sick. She had brought a book of family remedies with her and a small chest full of valuable spices and herbs.

"Mother told me how to make a poultice for his chest, Nathan. Mary will help me," Jennett said. The girls used a brass mortar and pestle to crush the herbs.

But still Josiah's rattled breathing coughed out in more irregular gasps, and he could not keep his eyes open. His mother tried to help the girls with the poultice, but by the time they mixed the strange mass of herbs, the small chest had stopped rising and falling.

Nathan rubbed the limp hands and put his cheek close to Josiah's face to feel for breath. But the boy was no longer breathing.

Jennett burst into sobs and hot tears filled Nathan's eyes.

"He was getting better!" Nathan shouted so angrily that everyone in the hold stirred restlessly. He covered Josiah's face with his blanket as Josiah's mother buried her face in her hands.

Now they placed the poultice on Mary's chest, for she had begun the same peculiar breathing.

Nathan had not noticed Edmund standing beside him clutching King Charles. "What happened to Josiah?" he asked in a quavering voice. "We had the pox and got better, Nathan. What happened to Josiah?" Tears flowed down Edmund's cheeks.

"Edmund, I don't know." He led his little

79

brother to their mother. "Stay here, Edmund. Don't move. And, whatever you do, keep King Charles down here. He might be a goner when the sailors learn this."

Quickly, Nathan yanked himself up the ladder and climbed on deck. He must find William Penn's cabin, or the captain, or Warren. Standing on deck, he realized the endless rocking of the *Welcome* no longer bothered him.

Several sailors sat near the hatch, splicing rope. "Look what dragged out of the hold," scoffed one of the sailors, moving toward him. Nathan stood firm.

Because the light hurt his eyes, he squinted. The wind whipped the canvas on the creaking yards. He watched the sails puff out in the breeze, drawing the ship forward, almost making him forget what had happened below. Nathan took in a deep breath of the damp salt air.

"Go back down in the hold, Quaker!" Three sailors moved threateningly toward him.

Nathan stepped back, wondering if he should retreat to safety and wait for William Penn to come down.

Another of the seamen, who was still whipping rope ends, said, "He's one of the boys who milked the goats and cleaned up after the animals. I'm sick of doing that. Let him take over again. Get over there, lad." The friendlier man pointed his knife toward the goats.

Nathan drew in another deep breath and summoned all his courage. "I must see William Penn or the master right away."

"Right away? So important, is it?" A couple of sailors snickered. "Going to tell the captain how to run the ship?"

"I must see the captain," Nathan said again, a little louder. He looked at the sailors who surrounded him. Luckily he did not see Drager, who must be above on watch.

"The captain is in his cabin with William Penn," the sailor who had mentioned the animals said. "Go ahead, if you think he will let you in."

Nathan swallowed hard, peering toward the door leading to the captain's cabin.

"That's the one whose mother and sister hexed the captain," one of the sailors commented. "Remember? His brother has the black cat below."

Nathan glared at the seaman who spoke. How could they think such a thing?

Another sailor muttered a fearful, "Aye."

Nathan's heart fluttered for a few seconds, then slowed when he reminded himself of what he must do. "I have to see the captain right away," he insisted, taking one step forward.

Two sailors with arms folded blocked his way. Nathan's heart pounded louder than the wash of bubbling water against the side of the ship. "I must see the captain." Nathan let his voice rise to a demand. "Or William Penn. I will take care of the animals as soon as I talk to either of them."

"Let the captain throw him back in the hold, men. Warren'll have our hide if we don't get the rope mended today." The advice from another sailor made the two men in front of Nathan turn their heads. He grabbed the chance to dash around them, throwing himself into the companionway that led to the captain's cabin. One sailor's hands had almost caught him.

Panting, he burst in on Greenaway and Penn discussing the route of the ship over a map on a small table. Though tiny, the cabin would be considered a king's chamber by any of the passengers in the hold.

"Young Friend Nathan, what is it?" William Penn asked.

Nathan grabbed hold of the side of the doorway to steady himself, trying to decide if he was more frightened of the sailors or what had just happened to Josiah. "The boy with the pox . . ."

"Speak quieter, lad," Captain Greenaway cautioned. "I've not let the crew know."

"He's dead." Nathan's eyes grew hot.

Quickly the captain, with William Penn right behind him, half-pulled Nathan out the cabin door and over to the hatch. The sailors laughed, thinking Nathan was the object of Greenaway's wrath.

The master ignored the ladder down. He jumped into the hatchway, held to the edge for a second, and let himself drop down. Nathan and William Penn followed him, taking the safer ladder down.

Already upset by the death of the boy, the settlers drew back from the captain, who had never been below. They stood around, huddled together, as Nathan led the two men to the Fitzwater family. Josiah's mother kept repeating what Nathan had thought.

"He was getting better. We all were. Why did he have such trouble breathing?" Fresh tears appeared on her face, and she turned to Nathan's mother and aunt for comfort.

My mother can barely stand up herself, Nathan thought. She looked thinner and paler than any time in prison.

Captain Greenaway noticed her, too. "Have you eaten?" he asked her directly.

She shook her head from side to side.

"You're having a difficult time down here. I'll have the galley cook some of your grain together in a large pot so you will all have hot food. You must eat, or you will get sick, too."

A grateful half-smile crossed her face. "Thank you, Captain Greenaway," she responded softly.

He gazed intently at the three women, then rubbed his forehead. "You must prepare the boy for burial. Sew him in his blanket," he said curtly.

His quick, cold order made Josiah's mother sob. Edmund and most of the other young children—frightened by Josiah's death and the ominous captain—added their tears to the confusion. William Penn drew as many of the young ones to him as he could. Nathan tried to comfort Edmund, leading him back to his bed.

Captain Greenaway tried to apologize. "I mean . . . that is the way we bury at sea. And if I can keep the crew from knowing . . ." His voice trailed off as if he guessed that impossible.

"We understand," Nathan's mother answered gently. "We would like to have a meeting on deck at that time, captain—those of us who can manage the ladder."

"Lie down, Edmund," Nathan suggested to quiet his brother. As he helped the little boy settle down on his pallet, Nathan noticed Jennett sitting up with her back against the side of the hold.

"Nathan," she whispered to him, "Mary and

Priscilla are sick. They have a fever."

Nathan clenched his fists together. "Do they . . .?" He couldn't finish.

Jennett knew what he meant to ask. "They don't have the sores yet. This could be something else," she said hopefully.

William Penn, carrying two of the younger children and followed by the captain, walked to where Mary and her younger sister lay. Captain Greenaway knelt down beside her.

"I pray this is ship's fever." He looked up at the silent crowd surrounding them, his brow knitted and his eyes narrowing. "I'll have the crew go to their quarters while you have the meeting on deck." He turned and slowly climbed out of the hold.

8

A FLOATING
PESTHOUSE

The captain's hope about ship's fever proved
wrong. Within three days, smallpox scabs
masked Mary Crispin's freckles. Her mother
and youngest sister, Abigail, as well as Priscilla, broke out. Fifteen other settlers became
sick, including the Tuckers.

*Two weeks of nightmare and at least a
month to go on this cursed voyage,* Nathan
thought as he dipped water from the large
barrel into a bucket.

All the healthy adults and children cared
for the sick, but in spite of all their work and
frequent meetings to pray for strength, one by
one they lost their Friends.

Nathan watched the Crispins, who had lived through Newgate Prison with them, become weaker and weaker. Their mother, Hannah Crispin, barely clung to life.

One evening hushed whispers came from the beds where Jennett, their mother, and aunt nursed their friends. Tears were streaming down his sister's face when she turned toward Uncle Thomas. "Our Friend Hannah would like you to write a letter to her husband and son."

Their uncle quickly got the paper, the quill, the bottle of ink, and his wire-framed spectacles from his small chest.

Jennett sank down beside Nathan. "She's going to leave us. They're all too sick—Mary, Priscilla, and Abigail. Oh, Nathan, we've been through so much with them. We all survived prison." She choked down a sob.

Nathan put his arm around her shoulders. "Barely. Only because Christopher helped us. If he hadn't brought us food and smuggled out our letters, we'd all be dead. That's what the men in power want—to get rid of us one way or another. We never should have boarded this ship." He forced his teeth together until they hurt. A rage burned deep inside of him as though he had swallowed a hot coal.

After eternal moments of whispering, when Nathan imagined everyone in the hold could hear the booming of his heart, their mother told them, "Hannah Crispin has gone to be with the Lord."

A whisper of wind from the gunport crack fluttered the pages of his uncle's Bible. Hot tears rushed to Nathan's eyes. What would they tell Will and Matt Crispin, Hannah's husband and son, when they reached America?

And what about the Crispin girls? Would Matt and his father lose their whole family without even knowing it? Nathan prayed deeply for the first time on the voyage, begging for their lives. *I'll do anything,* he promised, *if they can be spared.*

The women had already begun to cut a section of canvas for Hannah's shroud.

"Mama!" Abigail called from her blankets. "Mama! Mary!"

Jennett lifted the little girl's hands, wiping the bleeding sores with a cloth. Some of the scars appeared to have blackened all the way through. Though no one told him, Nathan knew the grim spots meant death.

No one deserves to die this way, least of all tiny Abigail, who was the same age as Edmund. Nathan could not move his eyes away from the oozing sores. He trembled, imagining the canvas of a shroud smothering him.

"I'm afraid!" Abigail's small voice filled the

hold. "Jennett, I can't see you."

His sister smoothed the hair from Abigail's sweating forehead. "We're here—Nathan and I. We will say a prayer with you."

Abigail's lips moved, and Nathan realized she was praying. The small lips moved slower and slower until they stopped.

Their bodies, weakened from prison and the continual damp and cold of the voyage, could not fight off the disease. *I should start a crackling fire in the middle of the hold,* Nathan told himself. *If the ship burned . . . good riddance. It was just a floating pesthouse.*

He felt like a moth trapped in a room, screaming silently, and beating its wings against a window until it falls dead. The world was a closed window to the Friends, and always would be. New World. Nathan doubted there was such a place. All the promises must be lies, a trap to get them out of everyone's way.

Jennett put her face in her hands and sobbed. Mother pulled her close. Nathan whirled from the nightmarish scene to the gunport. He wished he were small enough to get out the crack and swim away as easily and blissfully as a fish.

During the next long days of illness, William Penn worked tirelessly, nursing and encouraging the sick. His energy gave the saddened survivors courage to live. But soon some families had lost more than one member. Priscilla Crispin died a week after her mother and sister. Now only Mary was left. William Penn seemed to adopt the lonely sick girl, visiting her every day to comfort her. "I have never seen such a devilish killer," Penn said to Nathan and his uncle. "My sorrow for my Friends makes we wonder if we should have come. I had such plans for our new colony."

"This seems to be more than pox, Friend William," Uncle Thomas said. "Even Thomas Wynne has something keeping him to his pallet, but not the pox."

Penn knelt beside Mary, changing the cool cloth on her head. "Something else has joined with the pox, perhaps a touch of plague."

Colin MacKay joined Penn in trying to encourage Mary, and also Samuel, who now had the merciless sickness.

"I'm saving you a ball of chocolate, Friend Mary," MacKay told her.

She tried to smile, but after a weak attempt, tears dropped from the corners of her eyes. Gently, Colin wiped them away with his large red kerchief.

Because so few Quakers were healthy, Mr. Warren led the crew in helping them take the shrouded bodies to the deck.

Nathan heard the sailors mutter over and

over, "We should dump the whole bunch over the side."

One day Colin MacKay, who was helping Nathan carry a body to the deck, was pressed to the railing by three seamen.

"Cursed Quakers!" One seaman yanked at his cloak.

"I'm no Quaker, gentlemen, as you will discover if you press me another inch." His hand rested on the hilt of his knife; his pudgy face turned stone hard and taut. "Or if by some error you should tear my cloak, it will cost you a year's wages."

Nathan felt completely useless and scanned the deck for help. But when the sailors discovered that Colin was not a Quaker, and would fight back, the surly men drew back. Nathan's friend swiftly whisked him back down the ladder into the hold.

"Stay away from them, my young Friend. They're close to mutiny," Colin warned. "Still they can't take the ship around and gain anything, because we're halfway across the sea.

"We may as well sail on. Most ports in England would not let us come in anyway, with the pox. Lucky, too, they need the captain to set the ship's course."

Nathan nodded his agreement, but his body ached to the center of his bones, for without Samuel he had full charge of the animals. At least he had no time to mourn. At night he fell on his pallet barely able to roll over and go to sleep.

One evening Edmund paced the length of the hold and back several times. "King Charles," he called. "Nathan, have you seen him? I haven't all day. You don't think he went up the ladder to the deck? So many sailors go up and down all the time."

"He's down below looking for rats."

"He's never been gone for so long," Edmund reminded him. "Everyone is leaving us. I don't want to lose him, too."

"Go to sleep, Edmund. He'll be back in the morning."

"I'm going to search one more time."

Nathan turned over on his pallet. *I must stay awake until Edmund returns,* he thought, but soon exhaustion overcame him. The last thing he remembered was his brother searching every gloomy corner for his pet, even calling down the blackness of the lower storage area.

Ear piercing creaks and a spray of water hitting Nathan's face woke him early in the morning. The ship heaved violently from side to side. He fell the first time he tried to stand, and the second time balanced himself by holding the side of the ship. He heard the captain, Mr. Warren, and the sailors shouting on deck.

"We hit a storm." Colin struggled to sit up.

"Nathan, have you seen Edmund?" his mother asked. "When I woke he was gone."

Did he ever come back to his pallet last night? Nathan peered to the end of the hold and did not see his brother anywhere.

"Edmund!" He cried out several times, but only the groaning planks of the ship answered him.

Holding the safety rope attached by metal rings to the ship's side, he stepped carefully between pallets until he neared the ladder.

"Edmund!" His call echoed through the dimness. Nathan let go of the side to walk to the ladder, but a sudden lurch of the ship flung him helplessly toward the wooden rungs.

9

LOCKUP!

Reeling clumsily, Nathan grabbed for the ladder. His arms almost wrenched out of their sockets while he clung to a wooden step to stop himself from falling. A fine spray of water washing down the open hatch covered his clothes with a damp mist. Frightened cries, mingled with whimpers, filled the quavering hold. Deep inside the ship, the skeleton ribs groaned.

"Lie down, everyone," his uncle advised, but the pitching of the ship gave them little choice.

When the rocking planks under his feet righted themselves for a second, Nathan seized the chance to climb.

"Don't try. You'll fall!" Colin shouted. But Nathan must find Edmund before the captain ordered the hatch shut. During each violent lurch of the *Welcome,* he clutched the rope handholds of the ladder until his knuckles turned numb, waiting for the few moments when he could step up another rung.

At last his hands reached over onto the slippery, wet boards. He pulled himself on deck and was forced to stay on his knees until he found a line to grip for safety. Whinnies of terror came from the tethered horses, and the birds huddled together far back in a corner of their coops. Nathan felt sorry for the drenched animals. Slowly he inched himself by the pen with the squealing pigs and frightened goats.

The stout masts quavered like leaves in the wind. He feared the stays that held the masts upright might snap with each creak of the timbers. The bowsprit dipped until it disappeared into the gray sea, and then drew up, dripping a waterfall of foaming ocean back into the angry, warlike waves. Spray soaked Nathan's face and clothes until he felt wetter than the animals.

All around the ship, mocking waves rose and rolled as though King Neptune tossed in a fitful sleep at the bottom of the sea. If some hideous monster should break through the waves right now and swallow them, Nathan would not be the least bit surprised.

"Take another reef in those sails, men!" Warren shouted over the shriek of the wind.

Though it was wet, the rough hemp still hurt Nathan's hands as he drew himself on the safety line toward Warren's shouts. He looked up with shock to see men high above him on the yards, the long wooden poles that supported the rigging, faithfully obeying the mate's orders. With some rolls of the heavily laden ship, the ends of the yards dipped in the water.

By a miracle, none of the seamen fell in.

The captain stood holding tightly to the railing of the rear deck, crying orders to the helmsman.

"Keep her stern to the waves."

"Capt'n!" Warren roared. "We can't tack around! We'll have to ride 'er out."

"Take in the sails so the strain is off the mainmast," the captain ordered above the shrill wind.

The ocean mocked their efforts. They had no more control than a twig being swept down the Thames River.

Nathan's feet slipped out from under him, and he half-crawled toward Warren's voice astern, where the mate shouted, "Do you need a hand with the tiller, helmsman?"

A moanful roar of wind swallowed the answer.

"Mr. Warren!" Nathan cried.

"Nathan! Lad, is that you?" came a shout from where Mr. Warren stood on the captain's deck.

"What's that boy doing on deck in this storm?" Wasn't the hatch closed?" The captain's aggravated voice rumbled the sharp question.

Warren climbed down the short steps and held Nathan's arm to steady him on the slippery deck.

"Mr. Warren, have you seen my brother? He's missing."

Warren shook his head. "If he came up here, he's long gone. Look around you."

Invisible fingers squeezed at Nathan's heart. He refused to believe Edmund would come on deck. Still he knew how much his brother loved King Charles.

"The young one with the cat, Edmund, is missin'," Warren bellowed to the captain.

The master leaned over the railing. "Do you think he came on deck? He would not be so disobedient, not a young Friend. . . . Blast whoever left that hatch open!"

"He was searching for his cat, sir." A splash of cold, salty water forced Nathan to close his eyes. "He would go anywhere to find King

Charles." Nathan licked the salty water from his lips and wiped his eyelids.

"He's not here." A blast of wind carried the master's voice away until the chilling words drowned in the waves.

"Then I'll search the storage hold," Nathan insisted. "If he didn't come on deck, he must be below and if he's anywhere on this ship, I'll find him. . . . Will you give me a lantern, captain?" Nathan asked.

"Aye, take one from my cabin." The captain turned, his shoulders slumping miserably in the wind.

Soon Nathan had returned to the dismal hold with the light. The settlers gathered around the candle flame, like so many curious moths. Most of them had crawled from their pallets because of the violent rocking of the ship.

We are like moths, Nathan told himself, peering at the dingy crowd. *We are drawn to the flame that singes our wings, and we still fly at the light.* Nathan feared none of them would ever leave the *Welcome* alive.

Many of the children cried to see pox-marked faces so clearly. Even Nathan turned his eyes away from the worst scarred.

"Edmund wasn't above?" Nathan's mother asked in a trembling voice.

"No, mother. I'm going to search below."

Aunt Marjory held his mother's arm. For the first time that he could remember, his mother showed signs of weakening.

This cursed voyage. Nathan headed for the dark hatch that led below.

"Ellen." His uncle took his mother's hands, then called to Nathan, "I'll help you. I'll borrow another lantern and join you as soon as I can."

Nathan stepped down into the black hole of the lower storage hold. He heard swishing of water below, so he stopped on the ladder and held his lantern high. Several inches covered the crowded belly of the ship. The ship seemed to be pitching less, making his descent easier. He grasped the ladder tightly through one roll of the boat, then let himself drop into cold smelly water lapping at his ankles.

A scurrying sound and squeal made him jerk the lantern high.

"Edmund?" he cried, almost afraid to breathe. He sloshed toward the sound. His heart jumped when the candlelight reflected a pair of burning red eyes glaring at him from behind a barrel. *King Charles missed that rat.* Nathan backed away respectfully. He knew exactly how the cornered rat felt.

An ice cold lump knotted his stomach. What if he never saw Edmund again? Nathan prayed silently, then could not stand the clammy unknown terror any more.

"Edmund!" he screamed into the blackness.

No answer came, just the fearful pounding of water on the other side of those curving planks.

All the furniture, barrels, and chests still held firm, Nathan noticed, because they were lashed by ropes to rings in the side of the ship. He used these ropes to make his way through the crowded first section toward the sail locker, the small room at the very tip of the upcurved prow, a dryer section used for storing extra sailcloth. A short lash of rope tied to a metal ring in the wall held the door open.

The flickering light of Nathan's lantern startled more squealing rats. Goose bumps slithered up Nathan's spine to the base of his neck as the rats dove under the canvas. Nathan turned around and went back through the room where the hatch was. Slowly he made his way to the next storeroom, which was full of water barrels.

In the candlelight, the barrels resting on their sides cast flickering, shadow circles against the dark hull. Now a second light joined his, casting a dual set of shadows.

"The storm is easing," his uncle said as he came up behind Nathan. Thomas waited a few seconds before asking the obvious. "No sign of him?"

A wave of sickness heaved Nathan's stomach. He fought the choking terror by shouting again, "Edmund!"

The slap of waves answered his cry until above them he heard, "Nathan!" A weak, muffled answer pierced the damp air.

Nathan almost dropped his lantern into the water. Uncle Thomas caught his hand and saved the light.

"In that next storeroom," Warren's voice shouted behind them.

They found the door to the food storage area shut.

"Nathan!" Edmund must be pounding on the other side.

"The storm's warped it." Warren reached behind his right side and drew his knife from a leather sheath. "This door is always tied open," he said as he slipped the glinting blade into a crack between the frame. He pried it open far enough that they all could grip the edge tightly with their fingers.

"Easy now," Warren warned.

Quickly they all pulled forward on the door, increasing their efforts with each passing second. After several minutes of struggling, the door swung open and Edmund tumbled out.

A wave of relief swept over Nathan, and then he grew angry. Look at all the worry his brother had caused.

101

For the first time in his life he heard his uncle's voice rise above an ordinary tone.

"Edmund!" Uncle Thomas dove to embrace the drenched boy. His arms folded around his nephew and then swiftly drew back. "That's not water."

"No, uncle." Edmund sighed. "It's honey."

"Honey?" Nathan touched his brother's sticky sleeve.

"That's why I didn't cry out to answer you the first time you called."

The sweet smell of the honey made Nathan's mouth water. "You heard me the first time?" Nathan's hands trembled as he fought to hold back his anger.

"I came down looking for King Charles, and finally found him in here," Edmund explained.

The cat sat regally on top of one of the barrels, swishing his long black tail back and forth.

"The door was open then?" Warren asked, sounding puzzled.

"Yes, but it suddenly slammed shut, and everything went black. Then the ship began to pitch and roll. . . . I held onto the ropes that are tied to the barrels." Edmund's voice shook.

The seething anger inside Nathan cooled, and he began to feel sorry for him. Uncle Thomas held the little boy tightly until he raised his head off of his uncle's shoulder to tell them more of what had happened.

"King Charles chased a rat and caught it," Edmund announced proudly. "I knew he was here with me, but I was still scared.

"Then I got hungry. I smelled something sweet in one of the barrels and found I could pry it open with my fingers. I got the top almost off when the ship rolled and honey poured out all over me. . . . I licked the sticky stuff off my hands and washed them in the water on the floor, but I can't get the honey off my suit."

"If you were frightened, why didn't you answer your brother's call?" Uncle Thomas asked.

"Because I knew I'd be in more trouble than I've ever been in. I thought I might wait here until we reached America, but . . . I'm cold and I'm scared."

"We must examine your willfulness." Uncle Thomas quickly returned to his old self. "First, though, we will go up to see your mother. She's been very anxious about you." He picked up the honey-coated boy.

"I want to see mama, too." Edmund let his head fall back on his uncle's shoulder.

Uncle Thomas carried him toward the ladder. The candlelight from their lanterns glinted on the swishing water in the hold, playing ghostly shadows against the dark walls. Nathan watched King Charles follow them, leaping from barrel to barrel and from sea chests to the tops of furniture stored in the bottom of the ship. The cat expertly avoided any contact with the water.

As they were leaving the food storage room, Warren thumped on the water barrels, muttering to himself. He walked to the end of the rows of barrels, striking each one with his fists again.

"What's wrong?" Nathan asked.

"We've used too much water," Warren commented angrily.

"Because of the sickness."

Warren nodded. "It's my fault. I should have checked sooner. We've run low too quickly. We'll have to dole out the water carefully now, only for drinkin'."

"But we need water to bathe the sick," Nathan protested.

"You'll have to use sea water. My guess is there's barely enough drinkin' water to sustain us the next month, provided none of it's gone bad, that is."

"What else can go wrong?" Nathan asked. But he soon regretted his bitter tone. Mr. Warren had come to help them; he deserved their thanks.

"At least we found Edmund," Nathan said

to take the edge off the first mate's worrying.

"I would have searched every inch of the ship for him." Mr. Warren shivered. "At his age I was . . ." He paused, almost as if he didn't want to continue; then he seemed to change his mind. "I was trapped down in such a hold."

The gold ring in his ear flashed in the light. Nathan had always wondered about that ring. Maybe Warren was a pirate as Elizabeth Tucker had said.

10

A PIRATE'S TALE

"We would'a' been colonists, my father and I."
Now that Mr. Warren had begun his story, he
seemed to want to continue. The two men and
boys rested in the cargo room for a moment
while Warren told them more.

"My father and I left London after the
plague, the one where the whole of London
burned. My father had a mind to sail for Vir-
ginia to make his fortune.

"After three weeks at sea, we heard the
watch cry, 'Black flag!' My father dashed up to
the deck. In a few minutes he rushed back
down. He whisked me below to the storage

hold and pried open the nearest sea chest, threw the bolts of cloth in a corner, and tossed me in, tellin' me to not make a sound unless I heard him. That was the last I ever saw of him. . . . I waited and waited, though I heard screams and shook with fright. Then I felt the trunk move. Got a good jostlin' when they hoisted the goods up from the hold. Cried, too, but didn't make a sound as I'd been ordered, even though I almost fainted for no air."

"The next I knew the trunk lid swung open; the light was so bright I couldn't see for a while. When my eyes finally got used to the brightness, the ugliest men I'd ever seen loomed over me. . . . The good ship, where my father was, burned in the water a distance from us. I ran to the rail cryin', trapped and mixed-up."

Listening to the mate, Nathan thought how much luckier he was than that poor frightened boy.

". . . The pirate capt'n grabbed me. I kicked and fought, and he says, 'He's tiger enough to make a good pirate.' I hated him, but I was afraid. . . . He made me the cabin boy, and then turned me into a pirate. I hated him and lived for the day when I might kill him and be free." The mate's eyes sparkled in the lantern light. "Then my chance came. Durin' a boardin' he was about to be killed by someone else, which would have saved me the trouble. I don't know why, but I saved him and got my leg cut up good. He says 'What do you want for savin' my life?' and I says 'to be free.' The funny thin' was I already felt free—from the moment I'd saved his life."

"And they let you go?" Nathan wondered out loud.

"They doctored my leg as best they could, sayin' my use as a pirate was over anyway, if I lived, and set me to drift in the dinghy. Who should sail across my path but Greenaway. He knew what I'd been, but he took me in anyway, believin' my story. Any other capt'n, and it mighta been straight to the gallows for me."

Now Nathan understood Warren's loyalty to the captain. Still something else puzzled him. "Why did you save the pirate captain's life?"

"Don't know. I wished him dead for years, and when my chance came . . . well, I felt free, no matter what the pirates did. I think the old captain knew he'd lost his power over me. That's why he let me go. O' course, he expected me to die in that little boat. The maggots get some before they ever reach shore."

Warren's story both fascinated and scared Nathan, for it reinforced a suspicion that was growing within him that their voyage might end in disaster.

Even after they were back up on the settlers' deck a clammy chill penetrated deep inside Nathan. *If only I could be warm one night,* he thought as he collapsed on his bed. He pulled his mildewed blanket around his legs in a futile effort to get warm.

The other Friends were gathering together for a meeting, thanking the Lord that the gale had died, that Edmund had been found, and remembering Elizabeth Tucker, who had died during the night. Near him a pale-faced Colin MacKay struggled up on his elbows. "You found Edmund below?"

"Yes, Colin. I thought you were sleeping. Don't you feel well?"

"I'll be better tomorrow. The storm churned my stomach," Colin claimed. "I'm glad you found him."

Forgetting his own discomfort, Nathan tucked Colin's blanket around his shoulders.

"I'll bring you some water." He dipped a ladle full of the brackish liquid into a mug, his mind wandering to a sparkling, clear running stream, one that had gurgled near their old farm. Such streams ran everywhere in America. William Penn often read the letters of earlier colonists describing rivers so clear you could count the pebbles on the bottom.

During the next week, he and Jennett nursed Colin, who stayed to his bed. Between that and helping with the animals, Nathan went to bed exhausted.

None of the settlers had changed clothes since the beginning of the voyage. Edmund had not been able to wear his suit coat at all, and though mother rubbed the honey off with a rag, all of his clothes proved uncomfortable for him. They decided to trail some garments in the ocean and hang them to dry.

After asking the captain's permission, Jennett, Nathan, Mary, and Samuel, who wanted to stretch their legs on deck, went up to try the washing. Edmund wrapped a blanket around himself until his suit could be clean again.

"The light . . . hurts my eyes," Mary said as they climbed out of the hold. She was still weak from the pox.

"Pull your bonnet as far down as you can," Jennett told her. "You and Samuel mustn't stay on deck too long."

The boys helped them tie the washing to a rope. Then Nathan lowered the strange clothesline into the bubbling, churning water alongside the boat. A white wake as far back in the ocean as he could see marked the slow, bobbing path of the *Welcome*.

"Didn't you girls want to wash your dresses?" a harsh voice taunted behind them. Drager and another sailor laughed rudely at the suggestion.

"Maybe they would all like to take a bath," another sailor joined in. "O' course, the only water's down there."

Without warning, Drager yanked Jennett by the waist, ripped off her bonnet, and shoved her to the other sailor, who caught her arms. She struggled to free herself.

"Nathan, help me!"

Nathan hesitated, startled by the boldness of the tormenting sailors. He glanced back to find Samuel, his fast-beating heart saddened to realize his friend had disappeared.

He moved toward Jennett and Mary, who was struggling in the grasp of another sailor. In a most un-Quaker-like mood, Jennett stomped on the sailor's bare foot and kicked at his shins.

"Ow!" he hollered, letting go.

She ran to Mary.

Nathan tried to push the men away from them, but Drager's powerful hands tossed him against the railing. His rude laugh rang over the deck as he tore off Mary's bonnet. She screamed, twisting frantically, trying to cover her scarred face.

"Let her go!" Jennett demanded.

Rage clouded all Nathan's thoughts. Blindly, he flung himself at the laughing sailors. This time Drager shoved him to the deck. Nathan fell on a huge coil of rope, knocking the wind out of his chest. He struggled to catch his breath for a few seconds. Then he reached out for the ankles of the sailor who held Mary and pulled with all his strength. The man crashed to the deck just as Nathan heard a familiar whiz, the crack of the whip sizzling on one of the sailors' back.

Nathan gasped. The seaman lying by him had pulled out a knife. Quickly the captain's heel crashed down on the man's hand. He screamed and dropped the blade.

The captain bent over, picked up the knife, and ordered, "Warren, start the lashes with this one. Twenty!"

Clutching his shaking hand, the sailor cried in protest.

Another scream of the lash halted Drager's attempt to run off. Nathan realized that Samuel had brought the captain and Warren. And now his uncle and William Penn appeared from below.

"Nathan," Jennett whispered. "You won't tell them what I did?" He looked into her anxious blue eyes, remembering all he had just done, and with good reason.

They should not strike back. As Quakers, they were asked to be impossibly good, impossibly long-suffering. Though born to this faith, Nathan found it hard to understand. He decided the sailors deserved their lashing, and

he would be glad to watch.

"Don't worry, Jennett. Neither of us kept our faith." He almost smiled, because Jennett was always reminding him what it meant to be a Quaker. His younger sister had never questioned the demands he rebelled against.

Warren raised the handle of the whip.

"No!" Jennett cried out. She ran over to hold back his hand. "Please, captain. Don't beat them."

Nathan kept silent.

Immediately Mary joined Jennett in asking to spare the men. "Please do not harm them because of us."

The captain stared at the two girls, his eyes narrowing to slits. Nathan would not want to cross him now. But the girls persisted.

"This is not our way, captain," Mary mumbled between sobs.

"But this is the way of the sea," the master answered. "How else can I keep this rabble in line?"

"There must be another way," Jennett insisted.

Nathan wanted to warn the girls that the captain's angry face was clouded with the darkness of an ocean storm. But he just kept quiet as the captain signaled for Warren to begin again.

"Not with this bunch of dogs, there isn't,"

the captain said as Warren raised the whip.

"Captain Greenaway, my Friend, please." William Penn interrupted this time. "There is another way to reach men."

"Really?" Greenaway scoffed.

"To reach inside—touch their hearts."

"And is that what has brought your people this far—from the dungeons to this ship ridden with death?"

He's right, Nathan thought. Their faith made them objects of ridicule and scorn. The world continually blew against them, like the eternal west wind on the Atlantic ocean. All they would have to do to be safe was to renounce their religion.

Penn hesitated for a brief moment. "We have lived according to our own individual consciences. We . . . I have exhausted every means, politically and personally, to find this freedom of conscience in our old land or I wouldn't be here now. You know that. A faith that is not worth dying for is not worth living for."

Greenaway stared at Penn. Nathan knew their founder had been jailed several times for his Quaker faith, even once abandoned by his own father.

Nathan could not believe the captain's next words. "Confine these sailors in the sail locker," Greenaway ordered.

The captain had given in. A surprised Warren pulled the slip knot to release the tied sailor. The man fell on his knees in front of the captain.

"Not below the waves," he begged. "I'll take the lashes! Please!"

"Get up!" the red-faced captain spoke with clenched teeth. "I don't want to see you for the rest of the voyage."

Warren and the other sailors led the three men to get their gear from the forecastle. Drager managed a last, hateful glance at all of them.

"You see, mates, how these Quakers have hexed the captain." He pointed right at Jennett. "Beware of this one and her mother."

The crew muttered agreement, but none of them wanted to test the captain's temper. They backed away from him as he strode back to his deck alone, his fist pounding hard on the railing with every step he took. Nathan saw Samuel following at a respectful distance, obviously waiting for a chance to speak to him.

"I'm proud that you asked to stop the lashing. That took courage." Uncle Thomas put one arm around Jennett and the other around Mary.

Jennett glanced quickly at Nathan to see what he would say. His ribs sore from hitting the rail, Nathan did not plan to add anything to their conversation, especially that he would have been happy to see the sailors punished.

He wished he could help Mary, whose wide blue eyes brimmed with tears. Losing her mother and her sisters and having the pox robbed her eyes of their dancing softness.

"Do you really think there is any way of reaching the hearts of men like Drager and the other?" Nathan asked his uncle.

"I hope so. When we go below, we will have a meeting to examine our own hearts," Uncle Thomas suggested. "This is where we can make the most change."

Always the same answers. *Examine our own hearts. Study the Scriptures. Think everything out for yourself. Wait on the Lord in meetings.* Nathan wondered if his uncle or William Penn realized what the seamen had done, or if they ever noticed the real world around them. Nathan thought they lived in a foolish dream, thinking that men would change.

The rest of the day on the deck was marred by the early morning's incident. Once the clothes were hung on a line between the forecastle and the captain's deck, they all had to go below again. Early that evening the two boys went back on deck and brought the pile of soggy clothes below.

"Is my suit dry?" Edmund asked, clutching

the dingy wool blanket around him.

"I'm afraid it will take several days to dry, Edmund," Uncle Thomas answered. Edmund's hopeful face saddened, his lips turning down and trembling.

His wistful face made Nathan take off his own coat, which was as dry as anything else on the moldy ship. Sea moisture penetrated their clothes, blankets, and straw beds.

"You can wear my coat until your clothes dry," he offered.

"But that's too big!" Edmund protested.

Nathan rolled up the sleeves. "Look. That makes them short enough for you, and it's as long as your breeches. We can tie a rope around your waist."

Edmund sank to his pallet with a pitiful groan.

"All right, but I'm not moving from here until my suit dries. I'll watch for sea serpents and privateers." Glumly he rested his chin on his knees to stare out the gunport. King Charles curled up beside him in a fat, black fur ball.

Near them, Colin tossed restlessly. Nathan knelt over him. "I'll get a cloth for your head." Nathan found the bucket of sea water they used for bathing the sick and wrung out a small rag.

"That feels good, Friend Nathan," Colin

told him. "I don't have pox, you know. I had it as a child. My beard hides some of the scars. I'll be my old self in a few days. Do you think the children would like some chocolate?" Colin fumbled through his cape for the candy ball.

"Never mind that now. Just rest." Nathan saw his friend's normally red nose had paled to almost match the white of his beard, and yet his cheeks flushed a deep pink.

Mary joined them. "Nathan, your mother wants you," she said. "I'll stay with Colin."

Their mother sat near Aunt Marjory with her back against the side of the ship, holding a fussy Bridget. He patted the baby's warm, sweaty hands to quiet her. Then he turned to Aunt Marjory, who held a wet cloth.

"We don't know if she has ever had the pox, Nathan," his mother said. "She has no scars."

A dull gnawing bit deep into Nathan's stomach. "She . . . wouldn't live through the plague and prison and die now, would she, mother?"

Instead of saying anything, his mother pulled the bodice of the baby's dress down at her neck. Nathan stared. Bridget's neck was bare.

"We've looked everywhere, searched under every pallet," mother explained.

The necklace and jeweled cross were gone.

11

THE MISSING CROSS

How and when could anyone have taken the cross? Nathan thought first of Colin, who played with the children most of the time, especially Bridget. Yes, Colin had plenty of chances to steal the cross and plenty of pockets in his specially made cape to hide the treasure.

Disappointment overwhelmed Nathan when he turned to look at the man he had considered his friend. Had Colin only pretended to be friendly so he could take the cross? They should have locked the necklace away in their money chest when the voyage began. Somehow, Nathan would have to search Colin's cloak.

The sick man slowly turned his head toward Nathan. "What's wrong?" he asked in a weak voice.

"Bridget is sick," Nathan answered.

A low moan issued from deep in Colin's chest. "Not the babe! Not that one. Please. Oh, this cursed voyage!" He tossed in distress, with genuine concern, until Nathan managed to quiet him by offering a sip of water. Colin lay back panting, water dribbling through his beard and down the sides of his neck. Tiny puddles glimmered on the dark planks beneath his head where no blankets covered the flooring. Nathan thought he would rest now. Suddenly, without warning, Colin rose on his elbows, his eyes glazed.

"I must help care for her." He struggled to keep himself upright. "It is my duty."

"There's nothing any of us can do." Nathan could not hold back the bitterness in his voice. Twenty Friends had died and fifteen others were sick.

"Lie down, Colin. Mother and my aunt are with her."

"Call the royal physicians!" Other senseless words tumbled from Colin's feverish lips.

Nathan gently pushed his shoulders to ease him back. "Here. Let me put your cloak over you. It's cold." Nathan loosened the tie of Colin's rumpled cloak and brought the garment forward. That way searching the pockets would be easy. With one hand over the cloak and the other underneath, he felt the entire cape, inches at a time, but did not find anything that resembled the shape of the cross and chain. He tucked the cloak around the now-sleeping form and covered him once more with his blanket. He should be happy that he had not found the baby's necklace in the cloak, but the thought of being betrayed stabbed him with the sharp, paralyzing pain of a bee sting. He knew as a Friend he must forgive. Bridget's chain might be hidden in any corner of the ship, and Colin might never be able to tell them where.

He looked up to see Samuel standing over them, his hands braced on the beam. "I've been on deck. Colin isn't any better, and my father's still sick." Samuel sat down with his back against the sloping side of the ship, a frown on his thin face. "Nathan, I found out eight of the seamen are sick. There aren't enough healthy men to sail the *Welcome*."

"That's almost half the crew. And if the master gets sick, who will set our course?" Nathan asked.

"Friend Penn knows the ways of a ship," Samuel answered.

Nathan thought for a few moments. "Some of us are still healthy." He knew Samuel could climb the rigging, though against the dark planks his scar-covered face appeared paler than at any time during his illness.

Nathan went to his uncle. "Uncle Thomas, we can help with the ship. Samuel says half the crew is sick."

"We can offer, Nathan, and help if the crew will let us."

He and Nathan explained to several of the other colonists what they wanted to do.

"Let's go up and ask the captain." Nathan mounted the steps.

Samuel followed him to the deck. Gradually, the hesitant colonists came, unsure of what the men in the crew would say. Uncle Thomas went to find William Penn.

Captain Greenaway swung himself down from the starboard shrouds when he saw the group of Quakers coming. "I took a turn at the watch because we're shorthanded," he explained.

When Nathan spotted Mr. Warren on the top royal yard, he almost changed his mind about offering to help. Even on the lowest yard he would be higher than the roof of his uncle's two-story house in London. But they must help. How else would they find a port? If that meant becoming a sailor, he would try.

"We want to help you by taking the places of the sick men," Nathan explained to the captain.

The master looked at the dozen colonists, including William Penn, who stood around him. The tired lines at the corners of his eyes turned up slightly as he smiled.

"Mr. Warren!" he bellowed straight up. "Come down at once!"

Nathan watched Warren descend the swaying mast. Birds no longer glided around the dingy canvas because they were too far from land. In every direction they sailed alone on the sea, their only companion a single billowy cloud playing a game of chase with the top masts.

"We have some new seamen for you to train," the captain told Warren, without even asking the crew.

The mate accepted them at once. "First we had best show you the knots," he decided, concentrating on the knot used to trim the sails. He had Daniel, one of the other seamen, help him teach the colonists. "You have to be able to loose the knot with one hand when you're up on the yards. See." He pulled one end and the knot slipped apart.

Warren could have taken Bridget's cross. Nathan's mind wandered to the sick baby below. The mate came through the hold often, loved to pat Bridget's bonnet and say hello to her. Maybe he had been unfair to Colin.

Samuel learned the knot in two tries, but he had practiced them before, whenever they had free time on deck. After countless attempts, Nathan's fingers still fumbled with the uncooperative rope.

"You're goin' to fall off your place on the yard," Warren warned. "You'd better learn before we get up there." He pointed to the blue sky far above them.

Nathan caught his breath. He set his teeth and carefully followed Warren step by step as he tied the knot.

"There. You've got it," Warren said. "Now, me lads—up the ratlines. I'll set you five new men to the lower main topsail yard." He meant Nathan, Samuel, his uncle, Dennis Rochford, and William Penn.

The captain took the other settlers to the foremast to learn under the direction of the seamen who were still healthy.

Led by William Penn, his uncle and Dennis Rochford began climbing the ratlines on the larboard side of the vessel. Nathan admired his scholarly uncle's courage. This studious man was one of the older settlers—thirty eight at least—about the same age as the livelier William Penn. Uncle Thomas had lived most of his life in the city of London; yet he climbed up the ratlines without hesitating.

Nathan looked up. Six thick hemp ropes that were larger than his wrists, stretched over his head, finally meeting in a V at the crow's nest—the ship's observation platform high on the mainmast. The ropes, called shrouds, began below the rail in an extra board built into the side of the ship and continued through large metal deadeyes straight up to give support to the mast. The thinner ratlines, looped crossways through the shrouds, made a rope ladder for the sailors to climb to the yards.

The highest Nathan had ever climbed was on a ladder in their old apple orchard. But that was high enough. He remembered how, at a bellow from Mr. Warren, the seamen would scamper up the ratlines like spiders on a web, working the sails on the yards by stretching out over the freezing water on either side of the ship.

Now Warren motioned for him and Samuel to follow him up on the starboard side. Agile in spite of his stiff leg, the mate swang easily to the shrouds. Samuel took off his shoes and followed.

Nathan thought of how important reaching land was to them. *If Samuel and my uncle can do it, I can, too.* He pulled off his hat and shoes and jumped up the ratlines. Though the rough hemp splintered and dug into his palms, he held it tighter than he had ever held anything before. His heart beat faster and faster the higher he climbed on the swaying ropes. *Don't call them ropes. You're a landlubber if you call them ropes. I am a lubber,* he reminded himself, looking down enviously at his hat and shoes on the deck. His foot slipped through the ropes, dangling in air. Quickly, he pulled up on the shrouds to work himself out of the tangle. *Christopher would love this, just like Samuel.* He wondered what they were all doing now—Christopher, Will and Matt Crispin, and even Dog. Why couldn't he have gone with them?

Instead of almost running up, like Warren, Nathan could not relax his clenched grip on the lines and pulled himself up slowly. The wind froze his ears and cheeks and whipped his hair into his eyes until at last he reached his goal.

Warren and Samuel waited patiently for him, their feet swaying on the rope under the mainyard. Nathan slipped one foot out on the unsteady rope, then another, his heart beating so fast he thought it might fly out from his chest. To keep from falling he threw his arms around the yard. Warren moved in toward the mast, Samuel stayed in the middle, and Nathan—the last man—felt as though he were riding the end of a pendulum. As the yards swayed to starboard, he dangled over the rippling waves alongside the ship. If he fell now, he would drop right into the freezing ocean.

"Unfurl the sails!" Warren's voice boomed over the wind.

Nathan must yank the end of the knot that held the canvas to the yard. He would have to let go with one hand, and might either fall into the ocean or drop to the deck, depending on how the ship was rocking.

His feet swayed unsteadily on the rope. He clung for his life when the three men on the other side—his uncle, Penn, and Rochford—loosed their knots. Warren and Samuel pulled theirs and the wind whipped out the canvas.

"Nathan! Pull your knot!" Samuel cried.

Fearing the sail might tear, Nathan knew he must. He gasped, reached out, and yanked as hard as he could, immediately wrapping his arms around the mast again. With a loud crack, the sails filled with wind, straining at the lines as though they wanted to fly free like a giant bird.

Watching the huge canvas puff out, Nathan forgot his fear. The wind blasted his face from the starboard side of the ship, and he thought his right ear might be forever numb from cold, but he had done his part. Carefully, he inched

himself back to the shrouds and slowly descended to the deck. Warren and Samuel each slid down the side shrouds to the deck. The mate clapped him on the back so hard Nathan almost fell over.

"Well done."

"We didn't go very high," Samuel complained, his dark eyes shining with pleasure, color marking his pale cheeks for the first time in two weeks.

"Next time it'll be easier for you," the mate told Nathan.

He took a deep breath. Nathan knew now that he could climb whenever the mate called him—anything to get them off this deadly ship.

His uncle and William Penn asked the captain and the first mate to join with them in another one of the eternal meetings in the hold. Nathan climbed down the ladder, keeping his eyes up toward the sunlight where he had been. He smelled his last breath of the fresh, clear air and suddenly the sickening closeness of the hold smothered him. When the silent meeting in the hold began, his mind was picturing the sunlight glinting on the water. His cheeks almost felt the fresh, cold wind above.

To his surprise, Captain Greenaway climbed down the ladder after them and stood quietly to one side, bending his head slightly because of the low crossbeams. The master stood examining face after face of their company. For a second, Nathan's questioning eyes met his. Why are you here? he wanted to ask, but he dare not disturb the silent meeting. In the next quiet moments, Nathan felt a stirring in the Friends, with the slow, powerful force of a wave building up to crash on shore. These familiar seconds meant someone was being moved to speak.

Thomas Wynne removed his hat and thanked the Lord for his recovery from the seasickness. Nathan did not understand how anyone could be thankful after all that had happened to them on this horrible voyage. With a hope that ignored their situation, William Penn gave thanks for his land grant to begin this "Holy Experiment."

"Let us do our best in the unspoiled new land to make it a haven for freedom of conscience, where no man need fear for himself or his family because of the way he worships." Thomas Wynne voiced their hopes.

Penn spoke again, "Help us form a government with good, sincere men, for the best plan and laws will not succeed without them."

"And thank you for our deliverance from prison," his uncle said. "Give strength to those who are sick."

When the wave that moved them to speak washed away, the men returned their hats to their heads, almost by signal, and the meeting was over.

How happy King Charles must have been to get rid of us and pay his debts to the Penn family with some imaginary land across the sea, Nathan thought. Doubt about America's existence filled his mind. And if there was such a land, would they ever reach it alive?

As soon as their meeting ended, the master disappeared up the ladder. Most of the men took their Bibles and searched for cracks of light to read. Richard Townsend began to write one of his daily entries in his journal. His uncle sat close to the beam of light that came from their covered gunport, reading with his new spectacles perched on the end of his nose. He seemed completely unaware of anything going on around him.

Nathan and Jennett asked Thomas Wynne to examine Colin.

"He's not getting better and has stopped eating," Nathan said, setting a flask of water on top of his uncle's small money chest that also contained his writing materials.

"Our friend Colin does not have the pox," Thomas Wynne answered. "He may have the ship's fever. I can bleed him to take out some of the bad blood."

Weak as he was, Colin protested, "No!" and Nathan did not blame him. He never liked the ghostly look of people after this treatment, though bleeding was the most accepted practice for curing the sick.

Would Colin be the next to die? Nathan wondered.

12

A LETTER TO WHITEHALL

"Friend Thomas, would you write a will?"
Dennis Rochford asked. Uncle Thomas put
down his Bible, took the flask from the top of
the chest, and again removed his writing
equipment. His face grew taut as he took out a
piece of paper and quill and ink for the third
will he had written on the voyage. How many
more would he write before the *Welcome* came
to anchor?

Nathan decided they might be fortunate if
the world were flat, as the ancients believed,
and the ship would mercifully drop off the
edge, sparing them any more suffering in this
floating coffin.

Mary Crispin came for Jennett. "Your mother and aunt would like you to hold Bridget."

The girls left, leaving him alone with Colin and Edmund. Embarrassed because he still wore Nathan's too-big coat, Edmund stayed to his pallet as much as possible, watching for sea serpents with King Charles's help.

"May I bring you anything, Friend Colin?" Nathan asked.

"I . . . don't believe . . . you can help me," Colin answered in a hoarse whisper.

"Soon you will be better." Nathan did not believe his own words.

"No, my young Friend. I was a fool to accept this task. To be on this voyage is not worth all the land in the New World."

Nathan agreed, even though Colin's ramblings made no sense. A lump tightened in his throat as Colin wheezed with every gasp of breath. Even if he had taken the cross, Nathan could not help liking the once-jolly man.

"I am never going to reach my new land. Do you see it yet?" Colin asked.

"Yes," Nathan lied, his cheeks growing hot. "Your farm is beautiful. You are a great landowner now." He bit his lip.

"Nathan, can you write for me?"

"Do you want to write a will, Colin? My

uncle is writing one for John Barber, but he will be finished soon."

Colin wheezed a shallow breath. "I cannot wait. . . . I do not want a will. . . . I want to write a letter."

Nathan fumbled in the chest for a piece of paper. Of course, his uncle had taken the quill and ink. Colin did not notice, for he stared straight up at the moist, dark beam overhead. Nathan would remember what Colin said and later have his uncle write the letter or write one himself.

Colin whispered, "You have paper?"

"Yes," Nathan let the paper rustle so he would hear.

"To my brother, David MacKay, a servant at Whitehall."

"Whitehall?" Nathan gasped. The king's palace! Nathan's mind whirled with a thousand questions. Colin must have been a servant at the palace, too. What was he doing on the *Welcome?*

"I have watched over the babe, as I agreed, but now am too sick. You must send someone else. This is a pox ship, and the babe has the cursed sickness. She may not live."

Nathan choked back a sob. Colin's voice grew quieter until he could barely hear.

"My young Friend Nathan will tell . . . you . . . if she lives."

Colin had been sent on this voyage to watch the baby. Someone wanted to know what happened to her and had offered him land in the New World to stay near Bridget. Nathan remembered the man who had come with William Penn to save them from prison—the man he and Jennett thought must be Bridget's father or a close relative, the same man who gave Jennett an exact duplicate of Bridget's golden cross. Someone was keeping track of the baby. That could mean trouble for them.

Colin interrupted Nathan's puzzled thoughts. "Are you writing?"

Nathan stared at the blank sheet of paper in front of him. The story need never be told, unless he told it himself.

"You will send my message when you reach the New World?" Colin's hand groped out for Nathan. "The letter may take many months, but my brother will know what happened to me."

"Yes, Colin." Nathan held his friend's once-strong hand. The chilly fingers moved weakly, as though they had lost all their muscular power. Nathan decided he would send a letter when he could, telling what had happened to Colin. He would not mention Bridget. Reaching that decision, Nathan tried to search his conscience. He wanted to protect her and his family. Maybe Colin would get better. He watched the sick man's face becoming white until his cheeks glowed like marble in the dimness.

"I'm sorry," Nathan whispered to himself. "I thought you stole the cross."

"The crew was right, my young Friend." Colin tried to smile at Nathan. "Bad luck from beginning to end. But I have lived more life than many who have already been taken. Though my time seems to have been short, I am ready to go as all men must."

"Try, Colin, try to breathe. Would you like more water?" Nathan squeezed the cold hands.

"Give the babes my chocolate," Colin whispered. "God keep you through this nightmare, and may the New World be kinder to you than the old."

Silent until now, Edmund knelt beside the man with the special cape, his small face glistening with tears.

Nathan pulled the blanket over their friend's white hair. The folds of the material showed the outlined form of a man underneath, but Nathan knew he was no longer there.

"Why is everyone leaving us, Nathan? I don't understand."

Nathan did not understand himself. He felt empty and lonelier than he ever had in his life.

Mary Crispin, Nathan's mother, and several other colonists returned from a walk on deck. His mother held Edmund to comfort him.

"Will this voyage never end?" Nathan breathed in short, angry breaths. "Every minute of this has been wrong from the beginning!" He fought back tears. He did not know whether to cry or pound his fists against the planks that trapped them.

"We have hope for a new life at the end of the voyage," his mother reminded him. "Think of the moment when the *Welcome* will anchor."

He could not wait. They must escape the ship.

Aunt Marjory spoke softly. "I'm sorry about Colin. Nathan, we came to tell you that a ship is sailing toward us. The captain wants all hands to trim sails and drop anchor. He is going to hail the ship, heave to, and ask for fresh water."

"Colin was a good man. We'll take care of him," mother promised. "And, Nathan, will you ask the captain if Edmund may stay out of the way somewhere and watch?" their mother asked. "We need to go below."

"Why?" Nathan wondered. "To find some of our goods?"

"No. Drager and one other man in the sail

139

locker have the pox. Your aunt and I, Mary, and Jennett will take turns nursing them and the other sailors who are sick."

"You can't take care of men like that," Nathan grumbled.

"We must. The healthy sailors are too busy."

Her stubbornness aggravated him. "Will you please wait until I get back?" Nathan insisted. "I'll go with you."

13

AN UNLIKELY FRIEND

Nathan struggled against the overpowering desire to scream at the wind that blasted his face. He licked the salt from his lips and set his tongue angrily against his teeth. How could his mother help nurse those men after all they had done to make this gruesome crossing more miserable? Drager and his friends had tried to hurt Mary and Jennett and had made the crew think his mother hexed the captain, that she was a witch!

Nathan would go below only to make sure that the women were safe. With vicious jerks he tied the knot to trim the sails. Samuel moved over to check his work, nodded, then slid down the nearest halyard, a tackle used for hoisting and lowering, to the deck. Nathan climbed down, too, passing Edmund clinging to the lowest ratlines to get a better view. They waited for the return of the captain and William Penn, who bobbed in the skiff next to the other ship on the rippled emerald sea.

This vessel traveled toward England. She must have come from somewhere, Nathan thought, slipping on his shoes.

"The ship came from America, didn't it?" Edmund asked him from the ratlines.

"I don't know, Edmund," Nathan answered. *Does a province exist where we might finally live in peace?* The other ship struck a small spark of hope in his heart. He wished that they all might talk to the sailors onboard that ship. But even more than that, he hoped they would give the *Welcome* some water.

When the captain's skiff returned and Nathan saw the master's forehead knitted into a tight frown, he knew they would not be getting any extra water.

"Their voyage has barely begun," the captain told those waiting on deck. "They can't spare any barrels of water. I would probably do the same," he assured the crew. "We will manage with the rationing," he spoke confidently.

But the men muttered among themselves,

suspiciously eyeing the Friends who were helping with the ship. Habit, borne of those countless meetings for worship, made the Quakers cluster together. Nathan stepped back.

"She's the *Henry* bound for London with a cargo of furs and hides," William Penn explained. "When the captain learned of our misfortune, he did not want us aboard, but he helped us by taking our wills and letters back to England."

Letters made Nathan think of Colin MacKay. What should he do about Colin's request? He must ask his uncle to write a letter to David MacKay. And how much should he tell Uncle Thomas of Colin's mission aboard the *Welcome?* He knew his uncle loved Bridget as though she were his own child. They had saved her life. Whoever had abandoned her once, now wanted to know what happened to her in the New World.

"Is America far?" he asked the master.

"Many leagues," the captain answered. "Another two weeks or so, depending on the wind. The *Henry* will be faster on its journey, with the wind at its stern." He pointed to the ship already unfurling her sails to continue home.

"Tumble up, lads. We'll be on our way, too," the mate called.

Later in the day, Nathan went with his mother and Jennett to help the sick men in the sail locker. A rancid stench rising from the bilge water made Nathan try to hold his breath. Finally he had to breathe, and when he opened the door to the locker, the putrid air forced him to reel back. He doubted if he would find anyone alive when he raised the lantern. The light revealed all three men covered with smallpox sores, but still breathing. Nathan wished he were anywhere else in the world but here, where the very pores of the ship oozed with the deadly touch of a merciless killer. He felt like the cornered rat he had seen while searching for Edmund—trapped, with no way out.

Because of the horrible smell, his mother and Jennett took turns bathing the seamen. The stinging sea water they were using made the sailors scream.

"Mother, let's give them the broth," Nathan offered—anything to stop their cries. *No one deserves this*, he thought. He helped raise the men's heads to let them drink from the ladle. The men all looked like scaly sea creatures, gulping as they rose to the surface of the ocean. When the women finished, Nathan picked up the bucket and bolted the door.

"Don't leave us in the dark. Let us out!" the men screamed.

Their cries penetrated deep into the timbers of the old ship. Nathan heard them until he dragged himself to his own pallet and fell down to rest. When he tried to sleep, the pitiful pleas echoed in his ears along with the wash of the water. The irregular breathing of the sick made his head pound. His stomach rebelled at the stench of unwashed bodies, smallpox, and death.

If I spend one more minute down here, I'm going to burst, he decided. "Mother, I'm going to take the soup bucket back to the galley." He headed for the hatch, first checking Bridget, who mercifully slept. Old rags wrapped around her fingers kept her from scratching the smallpox sores.

Nathan ran to find Warren, who was standing on the captain's deck calling orders to the seaman at the tiller. "Starboard tack. Steady now."

"Mr. Warren!" he shouted. "May I sleep on deck tonight?"

Warren shot a quick, understanding glance at him. "We'll ask the capt'n when he comes up. But you can't sleep on deck alone," he cautioned.

"Samuel will come with me. I know he will. He hates the hold as much as I do."

The great sails of the masts flapped, filled with wind, and flapped limply once more.

"Tack to larboard," Mr. Warren shouted.

"Why are we changing direction?" Nathan asked.

"It's the way we make progress against the wind. I promised to show you, didn't I?" He led Nathan past the mizzenmast to the stern.

"Climb up to the crossjack if you can't see our path through the water from here. Tell me what you see."

Nathan saw that the *Welcome* zigged and zagged a path through the water. "No wonder we're taking so long!" he complained.

Warren's hearty laugh rumbled from deep inside his broad chest. "Watch what we're doin'."

Nathan watched the ship tack—turn to one side, then the other—to make progress against the head winds. He looked up toward the canvas, straining his neck to see the huge taut sails once more fill with wind and pull the ship through the water like the wings of a great bird. The ballast in the keel kept the ship upright and steadily moving across the ocean—dull old tub that she was.

"The merchantman we met will make faster time sailin' with the wind at her stern as she is. It'll only take her a month if she catches the right currents. But we'll still get you to your province. I promised you, didn't I?" Warren asked.

Nathan squinted after the *Henry,* already a good distance from them. The boat was leaving a straight, white wake in the blue green ocean.

"You've seen the New World? It's really there?" Nathan asked.

Warren's chest rumbled with laughter again. "It's there. I mean, the shore and the forests are there. I hope you like chopping trees, m'lad. . . . Wait, there's the capt'n."

Nathan stared as if Mr. Warren had drawn his lash and cracked the air next to his shoulder. His heart skipped a beat.

From the companionway beneath them, the familiar tall, straight form emerged wearing a black, broad-brimmed hat and a suit of Quaker gray.

"Ask him about sleeping on deck tonight," Warren said, with no surprise at all in his voice or manner.

Nathan turned to the mate. His mouth dropped open, and he knew he must be standing like a man who had lost his wits.

"Go down and ask him," Warren urged.

Nathan took slow steps down the short ladder toward the captain, unable to take his eyes off the man's clothes. Was he making fun of them? No, the suit fitted him perfectly and must have been tailored for him in London.

He filled his lungs with a deep gasp of sea

air. "Captain Greenaway?"

The master turned.

Nathan forgot about sleeping on deck. "Are you a Friend?" he burst out.

Greenaway nodded yes. "I was about to join the meeting in the hold. Would you come with me?"

"Why have you never said? I never knew!"

Greenaway put his hand on Nathan's shoulder. "Forgive me. I hid the truth, or rather omitted it, thinking the two did not mix—being a Friend and being the master of a ship. I did not want the crew to know. My men are the waterfront dredges of London, some criminals, others unable to fit into any life on land. The only places they know are waterfront taverns. Warren is the only one of the crew who knew all along."

"Why have you put on your suit now?"

"Because I have seen the courage of my Friends, you and your sister, Samuel and Mary, and all the others. I am ashamed of myself," the captain admitted. "I thought being two different people would make my job easier at sea. How wrong I've been. I've watched all of you conduct yourselves with courage on the worst crossing this weary ship has ever seen. Today I promised myself to wear this suit on land and sea. 'Tis a bad habit we Friends have of searching our consciences.

Would you join me at the meeting?"

An astonished Nathan tripped and stumbled toward the hatch behind the last man he ever imagined to be a Friend. Captain Greenaway could have waited until the end of the voyage to tell the crew. William Penn and his uncle and the other men must have known all along. He might have guessed only a Quaker would name a ship the *Welcome*.

How many times had Nathan wished he could take off his own suit and be like everyone else . . . so people would not know . . . so he would be left in peace without the tremendous weight of Quaker clothes? If the captain could change his suit whenever he wanted, Nathan did not understand why he would change now. What would the crew do when they realized the captain was a Friend? He may have put them all in more danger than ever.

"You'll be sorry you put on those clothes," Nathan warned so softly that he was the only one who heard.

14

DRAGER

A blanket of stars danced between the swaying sails of the *Welcome*. In a corner between the quarterdeck and the pen with the horses, the boys rested on a bed, as protected as possible in the dripping night air.

"Nathan, isn't she beautiful?"

Nathan knew Samuel did not mean the clear heavens, dotted with more stars than existed in dreams. He meant the *Welcome*.

No twisting of Nathan's imagination could make the ship seem lovely to him. Samuel should be anxious for their new farms, not admiring this ghost vessel.

"Out here you can forget all the cares of the world." Samuel folded his hands behind his head.

"This ship has robbed us of our Friends," Nathan answered. He almost mentioned Samuel's mother who had died soon after Hannah Crispin, but he checked himself. "I can't wait to jump off these planks." He felt a strange wall rise up between him and his friend. He did not understand how two people could look at the same ship so differently.

The damp salt mist soaked into their blankets. Nathan shivered, listening to the water beating on the bows. The honest barnyard odors from the animals, the bleating of the sheep, and the occasional whinnying from the horses reminded him of their old farm in Yorkshire. If he could wish on one of the twinkling stars, Nathan would go back to those happy, peaceful days. Those long ago times seemed foggy, dreamlike as though they had never existed. But he knew they could never go back.

Because of what Warren had identified as salt water boils burning on his face and hands, sleep did not come easily. All the seamen except the watch in the crow's nest stayed in the forecastle and left them alone.

When he finally dozed, a sudden cry from the watch woke him.

"Captain!"

Nathan sat up. He saw what had set the watch to cry an alarm.

Again the comet flashed across the sky.

The dampness around him lapped at Nathan's throat and chest, sending shivers to his arms and legs.

Samuel sat up with a yawn. "What's happened?"

Nathan could not speak. He pointed.

The comet appeared to be going in a different direction than in the sky over London—except that at sea Nathan knew he might be completely turned around. The awful sign did not glow as brilliantly as that first night in England.

Nathan grew chilled watching the slow, deliberate path of the star with the glowing tail. A feeling of dread, damper than the sea air, pressed on his chest.

The captain, Warren, and most of the sailors ran out to watch.

"We'd better get below," Nathan warned. "This will set the crew off." He stood up. Immediately a hand grabbed his arm. Nathan whirled to stare straight into the bearded face of one of the seamen. He drew in his breath.

"Don't fear, boy. We 'ave seen ye and the

rest of the Quakers helping with the ship, and yer mother and the others 'ave been nursin' those of us who are sick, and the wretches in the sail locker. We like the cut of yer jib." The man released his hold on Nathan's arm and stood back to watch the sky.

For the first time on their passage one of the crew had spoken kindly to Nathan, and when he thought back, there had been no violent reaction to the captain's Quaker clothes, either.

William Penn mounted the stairs from below, paying not a second's attention to the comet. He walked right to them.

"Friend Samuel, your father asks for you." The chill of the cold air clung to his words. Nathan glanced at the comet.

Samuel jumped up to follow Penn, leaving Nathan to gather their blankets. Dragging his feet and the clammy blankets back down the hatch, Nathan felt as if someone had beaten him. Samuel's father must be very sick or Penn never would have come for the boy.

"Capt'n," he heard Warren say. "We're losin' the wind."

"Aye, I see well enough," the master answered in a weary voice. The sails valiantly filled with wind, then collapsed, sagging limp and still.

All that night Nathan and William Penn

sat up with Samuel until his friend's father died. Almost one-third of the number who had so hopefully left England would never see the New World.

"God often calls for what we love the most and are least willing to part with," Penn told Samuel. "My own mother died just before our journey began. At times I thought I could not come with my Friends. But one day I decided that the best way to honor her memory was to build the dream into reality—our holy experiment—a province where all peoples would be free to worship as their conscience tells them. Your parents believed in that dream for you." Penn spoke with tears in his eyes. His deep sincerity and concern touched Nathan as well as Samuel.

In the morning, Nathan's mother stayed with Bridget while he, Aunt Marjory, and Jennett climbed down the steep ladder into the wet, black hold below.

"I'm a bit tired this morning," his mother had said. Since he was yawning himself from weariness, Nathan had understood. "We are cooking oatmeal today. That will give me more energy." Only once every three or four days were they allowed a charcoal cooking fire, because the smoke stung their eyes and robbed the tween decks of all fresh air. The women always cooked a large pot of mush, which would then be eaten cold until it ran out.

Once Nathan was below, he braced himself as they went toward the sail locker, trying to think ahead to the hot meal rather than the smell that would engulf them. No sounds came from the other side when he lifted the bolt. The stinking bilge water reminded Nathan of the garbage-filled London streets.

The hinges swung open with an ear-splitting, rusty creak. Jennett hung back. He held his breath and lifted the lantern high so his aunt could bathe the men. In spite of his protests, Jennett had carried down her own drinking ration to use instead of the stinging salt water.

"I'll be fine until the next ration," she had insisted.

One of the sick men tensed his body waiting for the sting that never came. "Has ye got more fresh water now, mistress?" he asked.

"No. My niece brought her ration of drinking water because she said you screamed so yesterday."

"Bless ye," the man gasped, tears pouring down his scabby face.

Aunt Marjory backed out of the sail locker rubbing her forehead. Her chin trembled as she moved into the tightly packed hold to take a breath of air.

"It reminds me of . . . prison." Tears filled her eyes. She had been sent to prison because she and her sister had made visits to aid the prisoners in the jail that had held Nathan's family and the Crispins. Marjory's sister had died in Newgate Prison, and she appeared about twenty years older because of the experience.

Jennett took her turn to help the second man.

"I'm cold," he said as she washed his face. "Could you find me another blanket?"

"We'll try," Jennett promised.

Nathan knew that if they had brought twice the number of blankets they could not stay warm on the *Welcome*. Why would they want to give any to these men? Only the cook by his smoky galley fire found any warmth at sea.

"There's going to be hot oatmeal today," Jennett told the sailor. "Maybe we can bring you some."

No, Jennett! Nathan shouted to himself. *That is the man who pulled the knife on us.*

"There's none for us," the man whispered.

"We'll see." Jennett shook the leather flask upside down into her cloth. "My water's gone. Nathan, would you hand me the bucket with the ocean water?"

Nathan lifted the half-full bucket. Nursing their own Friends took no special courage.

Nursing these men did. He wondered if his sister and aunt had more courage than he did, or was it something else? Something he did not understand.

"I don't need more bathing!" the man sobbed.

Drager groaned a husky protest, too.

"You'll fare better if we keep the sores clean," Aunt Marjory insisted.

The raspy breathing of the men filled the dark air of the hold. Drager's wheezing reminded Nathan of Josiah Fitzwater's rattling gasps just before he died. He realized Drager and the others might not have much time to live.

"Wait. I'll get some water." He dashed up the ladder to grab his own flask. Watching these pitiful men, Nathan had realized he no longer hated them or wished to see them punished.

When he returned, Jennett took the fresh water he brought to finish bathing the second seamen.

"Let me take over," Aunt Marjory said.

Jennett rose from where she knelt. Suddenly Drager's hand grabbed her arm.

"Let go," she cried.

"Where . . . where," he choked out, "did you find more fresh water?" Nathan quickly moved forward to yank the man's hand away.

Goose bumps traveled up his arm when he touched the scabby flesh.

"I used my brother's drinking water, too," Jennett answered. "He just went up and brought his flask back."

A hoarse groan swelled from deep in Drager's throat. He fell back, releasing Jennett's arm. "Curse you all! Why are you doing this?"

"Our duty to our Lord brings us here." Jennett spoke in a whisper, her voice shaking.

Nathan surprised himself by speaking up. "We will help you whenever we can."

Drager's moan filled the room. He seemed to be fighting a deep pain. His chest rose in short, quick heaves. "You give us kindness—your drinking water." A hacking cough seized him. Unable to speak for a few minutes, he finally gasped out, "Bring me my boots!"

"You cannot walk," Aunt Marjory said.

"Or breathe much longer. The boots I want. Say it is my last wish."

"I'll find them." Nathan dug through the sailcloth. At least the men's presence had driven the rats to another part of the ship's belly. Nathan found the man's boots buried in a heap of canvas in a corner of the locker.

Drager searched inside and drew out what he wanted.

The women gasped.

15

THE HORNPIPE

Bridget's golden chain and cross gleamed in the swaying candlelight of the lantern.

"You stole it!" Nathan said as he thought of the other men he had blamed—first Colin, then Warren.

" 'Twas easy. We came in and out for supplies often enough. I shut the young one in the supply room before the storm began, too. Saw him go in and cut the rope that held the door open. He and that cursed cat might have died there. And now you give us kindness." His words sounded accusing.

Nathan should hate the dying man for all

the pain he had caused. But he felt only sorrow.

"Why did I meet such as you?" Drager coughed again. "I never knew anyone like you before, and now it's too late."

"Don't try to speak any more," his aunt cautioned.

"You will forgive me?" This time the seaman's dark glittering eyes looked straight at Nathan.

Except for the pounding of the water on the other side of the bow, silence filled the candle-lit shadows.

"Yes." Nathan heard himself speak as though he were listening to a stranger. "We forgive you."

"Thank you." Drager clutched Nathan's arm. In a few moments the ironlike grip relaxed. Drager's eyes closed peacefully.

While the women went to tell the captain of Drager's death, Nathan carried the sparkling cross to Bridget. He was pleased to see her sitting up in his uncle's arms.

"Her fever has left," Uncle Thomas explained as he slipped the chain over her neck.

"Na-tan," she reached out for him. Nathan held her.

"I would rather have the babe alive than all the gold in the world," Uncle Thomas vowed. "So Drager's conscience got hold of him."

"Not his conscience, uncle. He didn't understand why the women were taking care of them. That disturbed him."

"I see." His uncle took Bridget back, saying, "Nathan, I saved a mug of oatmeal for you." Nathan greedily ate the lukewarm oatmeal, which had been combined with honey and goat's milk. He searched the bottom of the empty cup, wishing for more because the food made him feel better. He spotted another untouched full mug next to his sleeping mother.

"I did not want to waken her. She's worn out." Uncle Thomas's eyes avoided his.

Nathan peered at her. Even in the dim light an unnatural red flush colored her cheeks. Beads of moisture gathered on her forehead.

"She's just tired, Nathan." His uncle sounded unconvincing.

"Mother's never taken the pox. When we were all sick two years ago, she was the only one who stayed healthy," Nathan reminded him.

His uncle answered slowly, his face setting into a pale mask. "And when we were children I became sick from smallpox but she didn't. I thought her immune. Some people don't ever get the pox."

"Not many." Nathan pulled the damp coverlets up to cover her shoulders, the image of the comet blazing in his mind.

In the next three days, while the *Welcome* bobbed on the gentle waves, Nathan's mother became weaker and weaker.

Nathan decided the ship might continue to bob in the great Atlantic until they all died. He and Samuel milked the goats and helped care for the other animals while the crew mended lines and watched for any breath of wind. Looking over the sparkling calm water made Nathan's eyes burn. Waves slapped gently at the wormcrusted planks of the ship's side. In the air he felt an uncanny heaviness, as though the sea might be gathering strength for a final storm that would crush all their dreams.

The Quaker meeting that day prayed for wind and for Nathan's mother, the last person among the passengers to become sick. Why now, Nathan wondered, after she had been exposed to the sickness so many other times in her life? But if their prayers were heard, her condition didn't show it. She continued to sink further and further into a restless sleep.

Nathan and Jennett, Uncle Thomas and Aunt Marjory took turns nursing her.

"She will get well, Jennett. She has to," Nathan assured his sister.

He used his ration of drinking water to bathe his mother's forehead. He stroked away the beads of sweat that dripped down to the gray temples of her once-blonde hair. But as soon as he lifted the cloth, the feverish moisture reappeared. The uselessness of his efforts tired him more than the lack of sleep. He cradled her head up, hoping she would drink. Her dingy bonnet lay damp and rumpled under her neck.

"You have to drink some water," he insisted when she refused, moving her bonnet to a dryer section of the bedclothes and smoothing the material flat.

"Nathan, why don't you try to sleep for a while?" Jennett asked. "I'll tend her."

He eased his mother's head back gently to the floor, yawning and rubbing his own eyes, swollen for lack of sleep. "No. I'm going to ask if I can dry her blankets by the galley fire." Nathan knew that a line of seamen's clothes continually hung in the galley. He and Jennett exchanged their own blankets for hers, and Nathan took them up to ask the cook for the favor.

"Leave 'em here," the cook offered, shaking his head. "There's not much dries at sea." Nathan did not have to be told. He feared if he stayed in one spot too long he would mildew.

After he had helped Samuel feed and milk the goats, Nathan took the goat's milk to the children. Then he returned for his mother's blankets, which had not dried and now smelled strongly of smoke from the galley fire.

A weary Jennett helped him change the blankets. "Her fever's getting higher, Nathan. What shall we do?"

The more her fever rose, the likelier it was that she had pox. They would know soon enough. A futile glance passed between him and his sister. He decided they both thought the same thing, but neither of them wanted to say it.

When the vivid red blotches appeared on her once-clear skin, they were not surprised.

"I'm going to talk to the captain, Jennett. He's traveled all over the world. He might know another cure."

"If he knew anything, he would have told us, Nathan."

"I have to ask," Nathan insisted. When he knocked at the door of the captain's cabin, hope kept his spirits up. He explained and then asked, "Is there anything else we can do?"

The master's silence told him everything. Tiredness overwhelmed Nathan, and he sank down on the captain's bunk.

"Let me give you some citrus water. We give the drink to the crew to prevent the scurvy. If she can drink, she may become stronger." He handed Nathan a flask. "Drink some yourself right now. It won't do for you to get sick, too."

165

Nathan's lips puckered from the sour liquid. "Are those boils on your face hurting you?"

Nathan shook his head. He had forgotten all about them.

"I'll have the cook send you some broth later today for your mother." His face became more drawn and lined, and he seemed years older than when Nathan had first seen him.

"If we could get to a port . . ." Nathan began, then realized it would not make any difference. The pox was like the plague. He shivered, remembering the outbreak in London when they had found Bridget. Everyone was helpless, even the physicians.

On the forecastle deck two sailors with two of the worst voices he had ever heard sang while three others danced a hornpipe. One of the seamen, Daniel, saw the expression on his face.

"Not pleasing to the ear, I admit. We hope we sound so bad that the sea will want to blow us away," he told Nathan. "If we stay here too long, the worms will bore through the hull."

Nathan did not know how much of the sailors' tales he should believe.

The three sailors danced wildly until they dropped from exhaustion on the deck and three others took their places. Nathan rubbed his itching puffy eyelids. The boils on his face were beginning to burn again.

When he went below, he found his uncle speaking with Thomas Wynne about his mother. The physician examined her, but only shook his head and said what they already knew. "Try to keep her comfortable, that's all. None of the herbs have helped." Wynne put his hand on Nathan's face.

"Let me get you something for those boils. Most of the men who are helping outside are getting them. I know they're uncomfortable." He left and returned with a greasy salve that did soothe the burning. "Why don't you sleep for a while?" the doctor suggested.

"We'll watch mother," Jennett added.

"She's sleeping now, anyway," Uncle Thomas said.

Nathan settled down on his own pallet, next to his sleeping brother, and must have dropped off immediately.

He and Edmund both woke with a start when Warren stuck his head in the hatch and bellowed, "All hands! We need all hands!"

At first his body refused to move. Slowly he realized he must. The other men who were helping with the ship were starting to go. Samuel's bed was empty. He must be already on deck. Yawning, he forced himself toward the stairs. The fresh breeze cleared his head.

"We've got a wind, Nathan," Samuel called from the yardarm.

"The hornpipe worked!" Daniel rushed by to scramble up the forecastle starboard shrouds.

The captain stood on the rear surveying the whole deck, barking orders that the mate usually cried out because Warren was working on the yard next to Samuel. Nathan forced his protesting muscles to climb.

"Put the ship on the wind!" the captain roared. "Lively now. Tumble up, lads! Helmsman, are you ready?"

A muffled answer came from the man at the tiller, who must also have been awakened from a sound sleep. Men clamored up the shrouds on both sides of the ship to their yards, working rapidly to unfurl the sails and catch the wind that blew toward them. Nathan's own fingers grew numb in the cold night air. He blew on them to keep warm. When the sails finally filled with a crack of wind, Nathan clutched the yard so he would not fall off as the ship lurched forward.

The seamen cheered their thanks for the wind, but as happy as Nathan was about the ship moving again he could not shout.

"Steer her a course on the wind!" he heard the captain cry, which meant to tack as close as possible against the west wind. That way the weather-beaten old boat made progress with the head winds blowing at her prow. The ship obeyed in its own dull fashion, not glamorously, but steadily, with all the heavy ballast in her keel to help her stay upright. Nathan waited for the captain's next order.

"Tumble down!"

Lowering himself down the ratlines exhausted Nathan. He needed a good night's sleep in a dry bed. If he ever saw a feather mattress again, he might sleep for days.

When his feet touched the deck, he could barely keep his eyes open.

Thomas Wynne was talking to the captain. "May we borrow a lantern, my Friend? Jean Oliver is about to deliver her child." Below he saw his aunt tacking blankets to a beam to curtain off an area around the bunk and the bedrolls where the large Oliver family slept. Robert Oliver gave charge of his six children to another family while he stayed with his wife. Those not involved in helping milled around and talked among themselves.

In their small corner of the hold, Jennett was wiping her mother's raging hot forehead. His sister looked up at him helplessly. Tears sprang from her blue eyes. Her long blonde hair, untended for two days, hung in matted tangles at her shoulders. Mother had meant to cut their hair just before she got sick. It had not been washed since the voyage began.

"She won't talk to me, Nathan," Jennett cried. Their mother's head tossed from side to side. She mumbled words impossible to understand.

"I'm so tired," Jennett said. Nathan brushed the tears from her cheeks. "Go sleep next to Edmund on my pallet," he told her. "It's quieter there. I'll stay with mother."

Penn and Uncle Thomas visited them, their presence giving Nathan the strength he thought was failing him. Then their founder left to speak to the restless six Oliver children who were arguing about whether the new baby would be a boy or girl.

"My own wife is about to have a child," he heard Penn tell the children.

Uncle Thomas sat down near Nathan with his back against the side of the ship. Soon his head dropped to one side and he slept. Nathan no longer worried about whether his scholarly uncle would adapt to farm life. He knew he would work as hard as everyone else. His uncle loved the city of London, the bustling activity and especially the booksellers. He had not wanted to leave. But here he was, doing the work of a sailor whenever he was needed. Every disappointment in his uncle's life seemed to make his faith stronger.

Stiffly, Nathan sat up, hoping his mother's burning forehead would cool. He prayed for a miracle. Though every part of his body begged for rest, he could not sleep.

Nathan lay in a half-doze, listening to his family sleep around him.

"Nathan."

He started.

"Nathan," his mother whispered quite clearly.

"Mother, are you better?" he whispered back.

Her speech seemed clear, as though in one miraculous moment she had recovered. Nathan's heart pounded rapidly, and he almost shook his uncle's shoulders to waken him.

"Nathan, I never meant to leave you. There is so much I meant to do."

He choked back a cry of protest. "You will be better tomorrow." Nathan heard his own hollow words echo around him.

"Take care of your brother and sister. Keep them to our faith."

He leaned close to her. "Mother, it's hard keeping myself to our faith. I am not a good Quaker. I lose my temper . . ."

"I have learned, Nathan, that you don't have to depend only on yourself."

Nathan clutched her hands.

"Promise me you will do your best. . . . You have often told me you can work the farm like a man. You are young, Nathan, but you can do all this with God's help." Her thin fingers

171

touched his wet cheek.

"Don't cry. You have your aunt and uncle and many others of the meeting who will help you."

"I promise," he forced out. "But you can't leave us, mother. We need you. I need you."

"I'll sleep peacefully now." She closed her eyes.

Nathan watched her breathing growing shallower and shallower. He thought he knew exactly when her spirit left her tired body for the brighter world. He felt his own world suddenly slip away, like mud oozing through his fingers. If he should someday die by the sword, no blade could pierce his heart as sharply.

A gurgling cry echoed in his ears.

Nathan realized his uncle knelt beside him, tears pouring from his eyes. The strangely familiar sound did not come from Thomas. Wiping his eyes, Nathan searched the hold, which was bathed in an eerie glowing light from the lantern behind the curtained-off area. Again he heard the cry—a sound he recognized.

The wailing of Jean Oliver's newborn child filled the hold of the *Welcome*.

16

LANDLUBBER

Robert Oliver rushed out from behind the curtains. "A girl! We have another girl. We are going to name her Seaborn."

When Robert saw the expressions on their faces, he stopped. The happy smile vanished from his face. He knew. "Nathan, I'm sorry."

A consuming tiredness made Nathan tremble. Every muscle in his body ached. He wanted to run away, but his body would not cooperate. Slowly his weary frame rose, and without a word, he moved toward the ladder to the deck. With the numb, detached observation that occurs in a sleep state, he watched himself moving.

The fresh air cleared his head.

Without warning, the truth of what had just happened hit him. Tears clouded his vision. Praying for an explanation, all the time knowing there was none, he almost bumped into the captain.

The master's drawn face filled with immediate understanding of what had just happened. He leaned over the rail, speaking to Nathan and the sea at the same time.

"The crew saw right through Robert Greenaway. They said your mother hexed me. Well, she did." Clinging to one of the halyards he faced Nathan.

"No! She would never!" Nathan protested, wiping tears from his eyes.

"Let me finish."

Even through his own tears, Nathan saw sorrow in the depths of the captain's eyes.

"From the moment she insisted I keep the cat aboard and you piped up saying you could do the work of a man, I longed for what I had missed by being at sea—a family and a home. Oh, she hexed me all right." He bit his lower lip, probably trying to decide if he should say more. "Nathan, Penn gave me land in his new colony as part payment for this voyage. I thought of settling there."

Slowly Nathan understood what the captain was saying.

Robert Greenaway rested his elbows on the railing and gazed up at the rigging. "Perhaps I belong at sea."

Nathan glanced up, too. The thick shrouds grew smaller and smaller the farther up toward the mast they went, until they all merged together in a blur—a puzzle of rope lines, masts, yards, and canvas.

"Nathan, we're shorthanded on my ship. I would be proud to give you a berth. I've already asked Samuel if he would like to stay on the *Welcome,* and he has agreed. Your brother can stay with us, too, as a cabin boy if he would like."

Nathan waited before answering. "Captain Greenaway, I'm not a sailor. I'm a farmer, and plowing a straight row is a lot easier than climbing those ratlines. My family's farm waits for us in America. We'll stay together. I'll make sure of that." Tears burned in his eyes and ran down his cheeks.

"Then I wish you better luck than you've had so far, my young Friend." He took out a green kerchief to give to Nathan.

Samuel joined them. "Nathan, I'm sorry."

Why does Samuel want to live on this dull boat when the planks reek with our sorrows? Nathan wondered. But Samuel already seemed at home on the *Welcome.* In a way, Captain Greenaway and Warren and the other sailors would become his family.

The captain moved to the hatch to help with another shrouded form—the thirty-first colonist to die on the *Welcome,* Nathan's mother.

Samuel placed a comforting hand on Nathan's shoulder, but Nathan needed more help to support his wobbling knees. To steady himself, he grabbed the railing.

Once the shroud had been placed on the gangplank, all of the Friends and the other settlers gathered around in silence. The constant creaking of the ship and the pounding of his own heart drowned out the words the Friends said. Through mist-filled eyes, Nathan saw the faces of all the Friends except Jean Oliver.

Jennett and Edmund clung to Aunt Marjory, their faces red with crying. Next to her, holding Bridget, he saw his uncle's features, a pale, watery mask, mercifully hidden by the shadow of his broad-brimmed hat.

Friend Penn removed his hat to speak. "We come to honor the faith of one who suffered much and prayed for a better life for her family. She nursed many Friends and sailors, but in doing so she contracted the dreaded disease herself. She died helping others. I thank God for Ellen Cowell, for her love and devotion and the vision of God's love she has given us."

In the next few moments only the pounding

of the waters against the bow and the creak of the boat's movement through the water broke the unnatural quiet. Then other Friends spoke their thanks for his mother's life. Tears flowed down Nathan's face, but he did nothing to stop them. They were not just tears of sorrow, but also of love. He knew their Lord loved his mother. Maybe that was what he had been searching for: the sureness that there was something else—something beyond prison, the hold of this wretched ship, and all their suffering. At this moment, Nathan felt as if a crack had been opened between life and eternity, and he could feel the reality of life after death. Now his mother was beyond . . . free from all the suffering and alive with joy.

After all who wanted to spoke, two seamen tipped the gangplank. A ring of ripples marked the spot where the form slipped into the unfeeling sea.

Most of the colonists and some of the seamen stopped to speak to Nathan, but he did not hear what they said. He stood frozen at the rail until only Samuel, the captain, William Penn, and the rest of his family remained on deck. All the force he had left helped him to turn and face them. Jennett and Edmund ran to him. He hugged them and asked, "Uncle Thomas, would you take them below?"

His uncle nodded. "Won't you come?"

Nathan shook his head. He did not know if his feet would move.

Friend Penn stayed with him, telling Nathan, "We of the meeting will support you and your family in all ways."

Nathan wanted to be alone. He turned to the captain, "Captain Greenaway, would you let me stand watch?"

The master nodded. Nathan started up the ratlines, anxious to be by himself. He soon found himself in the tiny circle of the crow's nest, where he could still see the ripples in the water that marked the fatal spot more vividly than a grave stone. He wondered if the ring would finally grow as wide as the sea itself.

A light breeze sang in the rigging and dried some of his tears. Suddenly Nathan started, realizing that he did not occupy the crow's nest alone. Two dark, unblinking eyes stared curiously at him. A sea gull tipped its head to one side and then the other to examine the creature—Nathan—standing in front of it.

Nathan heard his heart pounding in his chest. "Hello, come here. Come closer." He reached out but the wary bird stretched its wings and soared gracefully into the air. Nathan watched it circle over the ever-widening ring in the sea.

A wind sang in the rigging, and Nathan recognized a scent on the breeze coming from the west. He clutched a thick, rough line to steady himself. His heart boomed with such force that his hands trembled with each beat.

Looking down into the growing circle in the sea, he thought, *That circle won't stop until it reaches the shore.* His mother's faith had carried them this far and with that precious memory his own faith would move on. Now, he knew why he had been sent on the *Welcome*— to learn to ride the west wind.

Men like his uncle and William Penn already knew. Like ships, they carried a ballast deep inside them that kept them from turning over in a gale. His mother had told him to trust God. Her faith had made her life worthwhile, and she had wanted to leave him that one gift, the greatest gift of all. No matter what happened, Nathan vowed that he would hold on to it. With God's help, he would see his family through what the New World had to offer.

The wind shook the hemp line in his hands, and he almost cried out. Blasts of the wind blew through him and carried the heavy bitterness back to the Old World, back to the past where it belonged. Suddenly he knew that in spite of everything—comets, smallpox, and whatever the continual west winds brought —this squat boat would anchor by the shore of the New World, and he would, too. He slid down a halyard, almost as well as Samuel, he thought, and in a few strides was knocking on the door of the captain's cabin.

The master opened the door. Warren and Samuel stood beside the table with a chart rolled open on top.

"I thought you were standing watch," Warren reminded him.

"I was, I am," Nathan stammered, barely able to keep what he thought to himself. "But I wanted . . . could I . . . borrow your spyglass? And, Captain Greenaway, I want to ask you a favor—about the two men in the sail locker."

The captain's eyes took the exact color of the sea, and when he began to smile, they sparkled like silver whitecaps.

"Mr. Warren, will you see the two men below are brought up?"

"Aye, capt'n."

From his sea chest, the captain removed a long brass spyglass. "You'll always be a landlubber, son. Won't you?" As he handed it to Nathan, he hugged him tightly against his massive chest. "You'll make a great farmer." Warren winked at both of them.

"We think that those who smell land first make the best farmers," the captain explained.

"Samuel," Nathan said, "you can live with us at first and try farming if you would like."

"You're a good friend, Nathan," Samuel answered. "I'll visit your farm. But I'm going to try a sailor's life first."

"We'll all visit you," the captain said. "This is almost the end of the tenth month. The *Welcome* will winter on the Delaware River. We'll clean her hull and pick up a cargo to return to England."

"Thank you for letting me use the spyglass, sir."

"My pleasure, and . . ." he said as Nathan backed out the door.

"Yes, captain?"

"You may call me Friend."

Nathan looked at the captain and nodded.

"I want to see what's going on." Samuel moved over quickly to join Nathan as he went out onto the deck.

Nathan scampered to the crow's nest with the spyglass tucked under one arm. He leaned against the swaying mast, put the glass to his eye, and adjusted it until the horizon became clear. The blurry outline rose into the distinct shape of trees standing against the open sky. Land! Nathan could see trees painted the riotous colors of fall—deep reds, yellows, and golds. Underneath that thick forest lay Penn's Woods, the Quakers' chance to try their "Holy Experiment." His mother and all the others had given their lives so that they could all be called Friends without fear of persecution.

"All hands to the yards!" Mr. Warren cried from below. Nathan handed the telescope to Samuel.

"The trees are beautiful," Samuel cried. "I see a sandbar—the coast!"

"Mr. Warren!" Nathan shouted down. "How long will we be to the shore?" He helped Samuel lash the glass to the mast.

"Those headwinds are growin' stronger by the minute. Depends on how fast we get to work. All hands, tumble up!" he bellowed.

"Lively now!"

Nathan and Samuel raced each other to find their places on the yard.

"Steer her a course on the wind," the captain shouted to Mr. Warren.

"Aye, captain," the first mate answered. "Mates!" he boomed so everyone on the ship could hear. "Tumble up there, lads! We're putting this ship on the wind. We've arrived in America!"